A Pekin Dewlap Mystery

THE
HAUNTING
of ELMWOOD
MANOR

Pamela McCord

The Haunting of Elmwood Manor

First Edition

Acorn editor: Shelly Stinchcomb

Jacket design by eBook Launch

Book interior formatted by Debra Cranfield Kennedy

www.acornpublishingllc.com

ISBN: 9781947392458

CHAPTER ONE

PEKIN DEWLAP WASN'T USUALLY the recipient of envelopes that weren't the perfect shape for a birthday card. The envelope she held was businesslike and formal, with no return address. She tapped her chin with her finger as she turned it this way and that. A letter that looked *this* important should not be unceremoniously ripped open. Sneaking into her father's study, she borrowed his long silver letter opener. Once alone in her room, she took a deep breath, opened the envelope, and spread the formal typewritten page open, smoothing it with her hands.

Dear Ms. Dewlap,

I was quite surprised to receive your letter regarding your services. It so happens that I am in the market for a professional de-spiriter for a property I own in Springdale at 12 Elmwood.

Please contact me to schedule when we can meet to discuss.

Elonia Collins

Pekin sank back against her bed pillows. "Grandma, I have a *client*." Holding up the letter, staring at it, her mouth gaped open. "I can't believe it. Can you?"

She hopped off the bed. "I guess I can't put off telling Scout and Amber now. Oh, Grandma, I'm so excited!"

Her grandmother had been gone for ten years, and no longer answered back, but Pekin still chatted with her as if she had a direct line to the afterlife, which Pekin suspected she did.

THE IDEA WAS SCARY. Exciting. Overwhelming.

She wanted to tell her best friends, Amber and Scout, about her new ghost-hunting business. Amber being Amber, she would freak out and say no way *before* Pekin could explain all the reasons it was a good idea.

Pekin had decided to do all the legwork before telling Amber and Scout about her big plan. Get her ducks in a row, be ready to answer any question or objection they threw at her. The next day, she would convince her friends how exciting this adventure would be.

Despite her anxiety, Pekin slept fairly well and was awake half an hour before her 7:30 a.m. alarm. She rolled onto her back and opened her eyes, nervous at the prospect of coming clean with her friends. With extra time before needing to get ready for school, Pekin propped up on her pillows and looked around her room, going over her plans.

Her bedroom reflected her personality, more practical than all fan girlie over the latest boy band. She kept it clean, her bed made every morning. Clothes were never tossed on the floor. She wasn't into the rumpled look. A full-length mirror was tacked to the closet door for examining her outfits, since changing her clothes multiple times before deciding on the perfect look was her norm.

Two posters graced the walls, both copies of the ones hanging in Agent Mulder's office in *The X-Files*, one reading "I Want to Believe" and the other proclaiming "The Truth is Out There." A white bookcase reflected her obsession with the paranormal, as it was stocked with tales of haunted houses and ghostly visitations. Ghosts weren't the only thing Pekin loved. Her bookshelves also contained a healthy dose of *Nancy Drew* and *Trixie Belden* books. Sure, they were popular when her mom was a kid, but they were still full of great ideas for teenage sleuths and fueled her daydreams of solving mysteries.

Her gaze fell on a photo of the three friends she'd stuck in the mirror of her dresser. She loved this picture. It was taken six months ago, and showed Pekin, bookish and nerdy, and Amber, looking short next to Pekin and Scout, her beautiful auburn hair wisping around her face. Then there was Scout. Tall, good looking in a Bill Gates sort of way, glasses, studious. And the reason Pekin loved the picture.

Pekin had known Scout since second grade (he was in third grade at the time, an older man), and this year he'd blossomed (if you could say that about a guy), shooting up three inches, getting contact lenses, losing the braces. Her heart plunked the first time she saw him after summer break was over and he'd come back from spending two months in Europe with his family. But *he* couldn't know about that, and she made sure not to let on that she liked him, not even to Amber, who would no doubt let it slip to Scout. Pekin would be so embarrassed if he knew.

Twirling a strand of blonde hair around a finger, she pondered how to approach Scout and Amber. Pekin wanted to be a ghostbuster. She wanted excitement, and imagined herself and Scout searching for ghosts in haunted houses. Amber would be there, too, of course, but Amber didn't figure in Pekin's daydreams the same way Scout did.

Still dressed in pajamas, Pekin wandered into her walk-in closet and inspected her options. Jeans, of course, but what top? She selected a white T-shirt with a big orange Cheshire Cat grinning on the front. She loved the way her hazel eyes popped when she wore it. Running her fingers through her hair, she turned sideways so she could admire the way it fell around her shoulders and down her back, then headed for the bathroom to brush her teeth and shower.

During her shower, Pekin considered her outfit, the one she'd picked for the day. Scout once said that the Cheshire Cat was his favorite *Alice in Wonderland* character. She hoped he'd notice her shirt and admire it the way she wanted.

As if. The three of them had been friends for *ever*. They'd grown up together. Scout probably thought of her as a sister. Just because she now saw him in a new light didn't mean he felt the same about her.

Amber had already started attracting attention from boys. Pekin was a bit jealous, but not about the other boys. She only wished Scout would notice *her* in that way.

Pekin stepped out of the shower and used a wide-toothed comb for the damp tangles of her hair, confiding in Grandma Virginia that this business was a perfect fit for her. She'd been obsessed with all things ghost for as long as she could remember. She couldn't count the number of times she, Amber, and Scout had sat in her family room watching scary movies or TV shows.

Pekin was nervous about meeting Amber and Scout for lunch. She'd been nervous pretty much all the time since she'd taken steps toward making her big idea a reality. As her planning had taken shape, she'd found it hard not to give off any clues that something was different with her.

The time had come to fess up.

IT HAD BEEN SCARY bringing up her brilliant business idea with her parents. Although always supportive of her, they'd both had concerns. Somehow, tracking down ghosts in haunted houses didn't go over in quite the same way as manning a lemonade stand in front of her house when she was seven. Her father had been proud of *that* venture. He'd even said Pekin had a flair for business when she sold double the number of boxes of cookies of any of the other girls in her Girl Scout Troop.

Knowing she stood a better chance of winning over her mother, Melissa, since she'd seen her share of ghosts in her youth, Pekin brought it up with her first. If anyone would understand, it would be her mom.

"What made you want to start a company?" her mom asked. "Why this particular company?"

Pekin glanced up, noting her mother's frown. "I don't see ghosts anymore," she said. "I used to think I didn't want to see them, but I was getting used to them, was finally ready to speak to one. Then they stopped appearing to me before I got a chance. I used to feel special. I didn't know anyone else who could see them. I want to have it back. That feeling. I want to be special again."

"Honey, you *are* special."

Pekin glared at her. "You have to say that. You're my mom. Besides, you know what I mean."

"Is that the only way you can think of to feel special?"

Pekin stared at her.

"I'm not saying no. I want to make sure you know what you're getting into."

Pekin shifted her feet. "You don't see ghosts anymore, do you?"

"No. Not since I was in middle school."

"Do you miss it?"

"Not really. It was part of my youth, and I moved on. In fact, I didn't think about it at all until you—"

"I'm afraid that's going to happen to me, Mom. I'm scared it's all over. I thought I'd be happy when they left me alone, but I miss being able to see things nobody else can. I want to help the spirits move on. But how, if I don't see them anymore? I can't go out in the middle of the street and ask if any ghosts are around. Maybe, in a real haunted house they'll talk to me. I bet Grandma Virginia would think it was a good idea. She was my first ghost, but even she doesn't talk to me anymore."

Melissa looked conflicted, and Pekin held her breath. "Maybe you aren't meant to have this gift once you grow up."

"But maybe if I work at it, I can make it come back."

Her mother sighed. "Okay. We'll talk to your dad together."

Her father was skeptical, but her mom helped to convince him. Pekin persuaded him that she wanted to do something impressive to help her get into a good college. What better way than to start her own business? The college apps argument was the turning point. He was impressed that his little girl was proactive about her academic future. Pekin was pretty sure he expected her to tire of the whole idea after a while, but at least he hadn't shut her down.

AMBER STRODE ACROSS the hot concrete of the quad to the relative shade of the maple tree. Pekin glanced around for Scout, feeling sticky and conspicuous from the nervous sweat she couldn't quite wish away, as she saw the focus of her daydreams heading toward them.

"God, it's hot today. I'm glad we decided to sit inside." Amber fanned herself with her hand.

"I'm going to melt if I stand out here another minute," Pekin said.

Scout pulled open the glass door to the cafeteria, letting them enter before him. "It's pizza day," he said with a smile.

They found an empty table near the wall of windows looking out onto the crowded quad and set down their trays. Scout devoured his first slice of pizza and wasted no time digging into a second. Pekin took tiny bites, careful to eat around the mushrooms scattered among the pepperoni, picking them off one by one.

She must have been chattering too much or laughing too loudly, because Amber said, "You're acting weird today."

"Weirder," Scout added.

"Oh, ha ha. I'm being my normal self. I don't know what you're talking about."

"Are you keeping secrets or something?" Amber asked, peering at Pekin through narrowed eyes. "I think you aren't telling us something."

Pekin choked on the bite of pizza she'd taken, and Scout pounded on her back. "Are you all right?"

"That's the classic response when someone's surprised with the truth," Amber said. "What's going on?"

Pekin coughed into her napkin and took a gulp of her drink, her eyes watering. "Are you trying to kill me or something?"

Amber looked back at her, skepticism radiating from her eyes.

"My voice isn't working yet." Pekin's voice was gravelly and hoarse. She cleared her throat several times and drank more water. "Why are you looking at me like that?"

"Oh, no reason. Perhaps because you're *evading* our questions—"

"*Your* questions, you mean. Scout, tell her she's the weird one."

Scout shrugged his shoulders, an innocent look on his face as if to say, *leave me out of this.*

"Thanks," Pekin said, glaring at him. "You're a big help."

"Hey, I'm Switzerland. You know, neutral?"

"You're *something* all right."

Pekin folded her napkin and stood up. "Anybody need anything? I'm going to check out the desserts."

"Bring us chocolate cake if they have any," Amber said.

Pekin breathed a sigh of relief as she heard her friends talking about something *besides* her.

She carried back a tray laden with chocolate. Before taking a bite of cake, she took a deep breath. "I need to talk to you guys about something."

"Okay," Scout said. "Shoot."

"I can't tell you here. Can you come over after school?"

"Um, why?" Amber asked, glaring her skepticism at Pekin.

"Because it's important," Pekin said.

"Are you in trouble?" Scout looked concerned. "What's—"

"Nothing's wrong. I'm not in trouble. I just need to talk to you about something. In private." She looked from Scout to Amber.

Amber shrugged. "I guess so."

"I'll order pizza," Pekin said. "Oh, wait. We just had pizza," she said to Scout with a frown.

"My favorite food. Don't sweat it. I'll be there."

CHAPTER TWO

THERE WAS A PACKAGE WAITING for Pekin when she got home from school. She bounced onto the bed and pulled her legs up under her. Ripping off the paper, she stared at the three boxes of business cards she'd ordered online.

Pekin Dewlap
Investigator of the Paranormal
The Ghost Company
No Job Too Small
Call or Text me at 555-339-6338

There was a set for Scout and one for Amber, 50 cards in each. She closed the box. She was hoping for more than one client. It was time to scare up some business, *pardon the pun*, she thought, laughing at her joke.

Over the previous few weeks, she'd taken several steps toward launching her plan. She'd ordered the business cards, created a website, and placed an ad in the *Springdale Ledger*: "Got ghost problems? Call The Ghost Company. Successful spirit removal guaranteed."

Unfortunately, when the only call she received was from her mom, Pekin realized she had some marketing to do. Where would she find ghosts who needed to be sent into the light? She pored over her website, noting the lack of views. Then she checked out craigslist. You'd think a community as large as Springdale would have at least *one* haunted house. Nope. An internet search for "ghost" and "Springdale" turned up *tons* of responses to "ghost" and "Springdale," but not *useful* responses.

If clients wouldn't come to her, she'd have to go to them. She'd even made a deal with the devil, trading doing Campbell's chores for a month in exchange for her sister driving her around Springdale to look for potential haunted houses.

WEEKS BEFORE, ONE BRIGHT AND EARLY Saturday morning, Pekin and her sister set out, Campbell grumbling about her chores. "You start today," she said as she tossed her purse in the backseat and glared at Pekin.

"*Whatever,*" Pekin said, while studying Google Maps and directing Campbell where to turn.

"Eewww," Campbell said, looking at the rundown neighborhood. "Why are we here again?"

"I told you. I'm writing a paper for school, on…um…changing societal norms. For my statistics class."

It was a lame answer, but it appeared Campbell bought it. Which was good, because Pekin didn't want to be distracted from her note taking:

"*1025 Parkhurst Way. Peeling paint, porch slats missing, boarded-up windows.*" Promising.

"9903 Rankin. Overgrown lawn, dead shrubs, peeling paint." And a For Sale sign in the front yard. Intriguing.

"*125 Martin Road. Not dilapidated, but looks deserted. Dead plants, stuff like that.*"

"I'm tired. I want to go home," her sister whined.

If Pekin wanted to be able to use Campbell's limo service again, she knew better than to push her luck. Letting her sister win this one was the best policy. Not that she had a choice, since it was Campbell's car with Campbell driving.

Pekin sat up straight and leaned toward the windshield. Half a block ahead she saw a tall, three-story house. "Campbell, go there." She pointed, her finger shaking with excitement, ignoring her sister's huff. "I want to take a picture of that house."

"I want to go home," was the response.

Pekin turned in her seat to face her sister head on. "Look, you're making me do your chores for a *month*. You owe me. This is the last one. I promise."

The car crawled to a stop in front of 12 Elmwood.

"Built in the early 1900s? Looks like no one's lived there for decades."

The number "2" was hanging upside down. She thought she saw something move in the third-floor attic window, but upon closer inspection the window was empty and she couldn't for the life of her pinpoint what had caught her attention. Even so, goosebumps broke out on her arms, and the hair on the back of her neck prickled and stood on end.

"Haven't you stared long enough?" Campbell whined.

Pekin snapped several pictures and started to turn away, but her eyes were drawn back for a moment. Nothing had changed. A shiver crawled up her spine. "Okay. We can go."

SITTING IN HER ROOM, Pekin searched online for any information she could find on the various addresses, including checking the County Recorder's website for ownership information.

Griselda rubbed against her arm, purring loudly. Pekin scratched her ears and grabbed the little gray and white cat into her arms to kiss it on the head, prompting Griselda to leap off the bed and run from the room the minute she was released. Pekin shook her head and laughed.

After that, she'd prepared and mailed letters to each of the addresses of the houses that fit her criteria.

PEKIN TOLD HER BEST GIRLFRIEND *everything*. It had been hard not sharing this with Amber. She'd been tempted more than once to blurt it out during the weeks she'd been doing the prep work, but it never seemed like the right time. And she was nervous about Amber's reaction. It would be better to tell her and Scout together when she could present them with their first haunted house.

It would be hard for Pekin to explain why starting this business was important to her, when she didn't fully understand it herself. Maybe she wanted something fun to do for the summer. Maybe she thought it would be a lark. Maybe she'd be good at it. And maybe, just maybe, she could get her ghosts back. Whatever the answer, her friends would be over soon and she'd have to give them a reason to sign up with her.

"And so it begins." She stood in front of her full-length mirror and sighed dramatically, a little shiver running up and down her spine. "No turning back now," she added with a trace of apprehension.

Chapter Three

WALKING DOWN THE STAIRS, Pekin obsessed over what would happen when she told Scout and Amber. She needed them. She couldn't imagine doing this by herself. Although she was pretty sure they'd be mad at her for not talking to them first, she could convince them. Whether it was starting a square dancing club when they were seven or a ghost club at eight where they called each other Ghosties and ran around in sheets with eye holes cut out yelling boo, or building a street racer out of old crates and bicycle tires, Pekin had always changed their minds. She was a genius at dreaming up ideas and roping her friends into being a part of whatever scheme she was interested in at the time. She smiled at a memory of Scout careening down the street in the rickety hot rod, trying to steer it around Mrs. Brown's elm tree that loomed directly in his path. Pekin and Amber ran after him screaming and laughing and waving their hands in the air. Luckily for Scout, he managed to veer off enough to miss the tree and plowed into a relatively soft bunch of begonias instead. No harm done.

Her two sidekicks might not have been as into the paranormal as she was, but she tried to include them as she indulged her never-ending interest in ghosts. Pekin didn't have any trouble convincing them to hang out at her house for pizza and spooky movies. They teased her when she told them she wanted to start a ghostbusting business someday, something she brought up more than once.

"I wanna be president," Scout said with a grin.

"Fat chance," Pekin responded.

As they got older, however, there were more interesting ways for teenagers to spend their time than being immersed in ghost stories. Pekin could see things were changing, and it made her sad sometimes.

She needed to do something before she lost her friends to pursuits more normal for high school students. She hoped her business venture would bring her friends back into the fold. Or maybe not. If not, maybe it was time for Pekin to move on as well.

Chapter Four

B EFORE PEKIN REACHED THE BOTTOM STEP, the doorbell rang. Scout's tall form was visible through the wavy yellow glass in the top half of the front door. Pekin squared her shoulders and pasted a smile on her face. With one final anxious adjustment to her ponytail, Pekin let him in.

"Why are you grinning?" Scout asked, scrutinizing Pekin's face. "You look like you ate a canary. Is the pizza here yet?" Over his shoulder, Pekin saw Amber coming up the walk.

She put her hands on her hips and glared up at Scout. "You just got here. We have to talk. Pizza later."

"Talk about what?" he asked.

"Yeah, why exactly are we here?" Amber asked.

Pekin cleared her throat as she ushered them into the den and waited for them to plop onto the sofa. She looked solemnly from one friend to the other. "You know how we've all been into ghosts and paranormal stuff?"

"Well, maybe that would be you more than us," Amber said.

"I think you were driving that bus, Pekie," Scout added.

"Whatever. The point is I didn't tell you this before but I can see ghosts."

"Sure you can. I saw the Loch Ness Monster on my vacation last summer."

Pekin shot him a glare. "You did not. And stop trying to make fun of me. I really can see ghosts."

"And this is the first we're hearing about it? Sounds a little fishy to me."

"If that's true, how come you never told us before?" Amber asked.

"Because. For one thing, my mom said it would make me seem weird."

"Too late for that," Amber said.

"Are there any ghosts in the room with us?" Scout asked.

"No there aren't," Pekin said, rolling her eyes. "Look, I know this is coming out of nowhere since this is the first you're hearing it, but it's true. When I was five, right after my grandma died, I saw her in my room. I loved my grandma and was happy when her spirit would visit me now and then. I was never scared. Then, in first grade, a ghost approached me. Only, I didn't know it was a ghost until Laura Jenkins walked right through him. Now, that? That scared the pants off me. As soon as I got home from school, I told my mom. Check this out, she totally believed me! She said the ghost didn't want to hurt me and that I'd probably see more of them. Turns out my mom had her own experiences seeing ghosts when she was younger. She warned me not to let the ghosts know I could see them because I'd be bombarded with spirits needing help. If the boy on the playground hadn't scared me enough, my mom's words did. I took her advice and pretended not to see them. But, eventually, I really did stop seeing them, and I miss them."

Amber's eyes grew wide. "Was your grandma here any of the times I've stayed the night?"

"Seriously Amber? I tell you I can see ghosts and you're worried about whether my sweet grandma was here at the same time as you?"

"Anyway," Scout said, obviously trying to get the conversation back on track, "what does this have to do with me and Amber? What was it you wanted to talk to us about?"

"I'm starting a new business and I want to recruit you. It will be called 'The Ghost Company.'"

She held up her hand to interrupt the questions and eye-rolling she could see forming. "I'll be the president, of course, since it's my idea, but you'll be my investigators."

"Investigators of what?" Scout asked.

"Yeah, what?" Amber contributed.

"I need you guys. You're my Jim and Honey, my Helen and Bess and George, my—"

"Your who?" Scout looked genuinely puzzled.

"You know, *Trixie Belden*, *Nancy Drew*. Don't you read?"

"That's girl stuff."

"It's *mystery* stuff."

"Yeah, yeah." Scout picked up the remote and clicked on the TV.

"Scout." Pekin frowned. "Turn that off."

She took the remote out of his hand and clicked the TV off. "This is important." She stood with her arms crossed trying to look stern.

Her friends waited.

"I'm starting a business and I need assistants. That would be you guys, my best friends in the whole world."

As Amber opened her mouth to speak, Pekin hurried on. "We are going to help Springdale get rid of its ghosts." She paused. "Ta DAH!"

Scout rolled his eyes and pushed off the sofa. "Got anything to eat while we wait for the pizza?"

Amber stood, too, but thoughtfully said, "Pekin, I'm sure that's a great offer, but I don't *like* ghosts," before following Scout out of the room.

"But I *need* you," she shouted after them.

A minute later, Scout and Amber returned to the sofa, each with a Pepsi and a bag of chips.

Pekin felt deflated. The weight of her failed pitch crashed around her ears. She quickly realized where she'd gone wrong. "I'm sorry," she said. "I guess I got carried away. I assumed—Wait. No, I *hoped* that you'd want to do this with me."

The room was silent. Amber looked stunned and Scout looked dumbfounded.

"Wait a minute. You're serious about this?" he asked.

"Well, I *was*. I mean, couldn't you try it to see if you like it?"

No one jumped at the suggestion. "I did a lot of work already. I wanted all the details to be worked out before I told you everything. I wanted it to be *real* before I told you about it. I took pictures, and ordered business cards—"

She handed each of them a box of cards. "Here."

"Why would we want in on this?" Scout asked, popping a chip into his mouth.

"Because it's exciting. It will be fun."

"I don't think ghosts are fun," Amber said.

"Okay. How about this? Think about how good running your own business will look on your college apps. This is the *perfect* extra-curricular. It's thought-provoking. Unique. Not your run-of-the-mill business."

"I'm not going to worry about college until next year," Amber said.

"First of all, we wouldn't be running our own business," Scout said. "We'd be working for you. So, while it might look good on *your* apps, it wouldn't do much for ours."

Pekin tapped her chin with her finger. "Hmmm. I hadn't thought of it that way. We're still in the planning stages. We can all be co-owners. There. It's done."

"I don't think I want to be a co-owner," Amber whined.

"*Amber*. Work with me here. I'm trying to sweeten the deal for you guys. Look what I've done already." She opened her notebook and leafed through the pages.

She flipped to the "12 Elmwood" tab. "This house is the most promising. I mean, look at it. Doesn't it scream 'haunted' to you?"

Amber peered at it. "It's creepy." She passed the notebook to Scout who, with a frown, glanced at the photos and immediately turned his attention back to the bag of chips.

"Scout, really?" Pekin scolded. "Get your head in the game. Can't you see how eerie that house is?"

"What do you want me to say? All right. The house looks spooky. Creepy, actually, like Amber said. Now what?"

"I wrote to the owner and she replied."

"You what?" Amber looked horrified. "The owner has to think you're a crazy person."

"She doesn't. And I'm not a crazy person." Pekin pulled the letter out of her back pocket. "Here. See for yourself. Elonia Collins said she has a spirit problem."

Scout took the letter from Pekin, read it and handed it back.

"Once the ghost is gone, then someone can fix the house up and a nice family can move in. No family would want to live there now.

Think of the good we'd be doing for Ms. Collins."

"No family would want to live in that house even if there were *no* ghosts," Amber said.

"All it needs is a little TLC. But that's not our focus."

"You mean that's not *your* focus."

"Aren't you guys interested in being my co-owners? In a *real business?*"

"I still don't like ghosts," Amber said.

"Oh my God, Amber. Don't be such a baby. This is an adventure."

"Don't pick on Amber," Scout said sharply, looking up from the TV.

"I'm not picking on anyone. Is it a crime to want my best friends to show even a *speck* of interest in my plan? Unfortunately, neither of you can be bothered. I guess I made a mistake thinking you'd want to do this with me."

Scout must have noticed how deflated Pekin felt because he put down the TV remote and held out his hand. "Let me take a look at your research."

"Really?" She handed him the notebook, feeling grateful that he was willing to consider her proposal.

Scout turned the pages and Amber leaned over Pekin so she could see, too.

Pekin smiled a little smile to herself. Daring to hope.

The doorbell chimed. "Pizza," Scout said with a grin, jumping up, handing Pekin the notebook and heading for the front door. "Finally!"

Amber spread out paper plates on the coffee table as Scout opened the box. He sat back on the sofa, dramatically rubbing his hands together. Business cards, ghosts and Pekin's business plan forgotten in favor of watching *The Vampire Diaries*. Within moments, he and Amber were engrossed in the lives, make that non-lives, of Elena, Damon, Stefan and the rest of their undead friends.

It took some prodding to convince her friends to take their boxes of business cards with them. Baby steps, Pekin thought. We have to take baby steps.

CHAPTER FIVE

WITH AMBER AND SCOUT now in the know, Pekin wasted no time texting Elonia to express her enthusiasm about removing the ghost from 12 Elmwood. They agreed to meet Saturday at noon at Cracker Barrel. Pekin almost suggested meeting at the Elmwood house, but didn't want to scare her friends off before they got started. Even Pekin felt a little tickle of fear, overwhelmed at the thought of meeting Elonia in person.

She texted Amber. When she didn't get a text back in five minutes, she dialed Amber's phone.

"What's up, Pekin?"

"You didn't answer my text."

"Because I was helping my mom with dinner. What's the rush?"

"Elonia texted me. We're meeting her Saturday."

"Oh."

Pekin could hear her friend's reluctance over the phone. "You're going with me, aren't you?"

"Um," Amber started, then sighed. "Did you tell Scout?"

"Not yet. I'll tell him at school tomorrow. I'm going to be too excited to sleep."

"I'm not sure I'll get any sleep either. And it won't be because I'm too excited," Amber said.

Chapter Six

"HOW MUCH TIME is this going to take?" Scout asked, frowning. "I mean, I have practice after school most days. And other stuff."

Amber hadn't joined them at their usual lunch spot in the quad yet, giving Pekin time to break down Scout's resistance. She couldn't let him weasel out on her before they'd even begun.

"We won't know 'til we meet with Elonia on Saturday. I can count on you, right? Otherwise, I don't think my parents will let me meet with her, because she's a *stranger*. They can be really lame sometimes."

"Well, I—"

"You *have* to be there, Scout." She looked up at him and made her most pleading face.

"Oh, God, Pekin. *Fine*."

"Thank you. I knew I could count on you." She spotted Amber over Scout's shoulder and waved, scooting over on the bench to make room for her friend.

"Scout's in for Saturday," Pekin said, using her most enthusiastic voice. She had to give Amber props for the *Yay Team* kind of smile that she couldn't quite pull off. Amber always did her best to be supportive, even if it took a superhuman effort.

"It's going to be fun, Amber," Pekin said. "You'll see."

"I'm sure," Amber said, as she set down her lunch tray. "I can't wait."

SATURDAY MORNING, PEKIN BALANCED her laptop on her knees and set about writing down talking points to discuss with her new client. With that done, she spent an hour selecting and deselecting outfits. Pekin wanted to appear mature and capable. The trouble was, she didn't have a lot of clothes that would pull off the mature and capable look. What 15-year old did? A closet full of cutoffs and tank tops and flip flops wouldn't cut it. She settled on her nicest jeans and a yellow cotton sweater. Turning back and forth in front of the mirror, she pulled off the yellow sweater and replaced it with a more toned-down, light-weight green one. It wouldn't do to look frivolous, she decided.

She pulled her long ash blonde hair up into a ponytail and brushed a touch of mascara on her fringe of lashes. She wondered if Scout would think she looked nice. Maybe it was a good thing Amber had begged off at the last minute, claiming a family obligation. Then Pekin was horrified at the thought of being happy that Amber was missing the meeting. She needed *both* of her best friends.

As if she wasn't nervous enough, Scout was late. Pekin stood on the front porch alternately tapping her foot and looking at the time on her phone. When his white Corolla, with a slightly dented front bumper, rolled up to the curb in front of her house, Pekin had to bite her tongue to keep from launching into a speech about punctuality. The look on her face was sufficient, however, for Scout to say, "Geez, Pekin. I'm only five minutes late. Give it a break."

Pekin sighed loudly. "Of course. How silly of me to be concerned that our very first customer, I mean *client*, might frown at our inability to show up on time." She harrumphed and crossed her arms over her chest as she scrunched down in the front seat of his car.

When he didn't immediately drive away, she looked up to see him staring at her. "What?" she asked grumpily.

"You're too much, you know that?"

Pekin took a breath. And then another one. She didn't often get irritated with Scout. In other circumstances, she'd be thrilled to be alone, in a car, with the object of her crush. And he *was* going with her, after all. He hadn't bailed like Amber did. "I'm sorry, Scout. I'm just really *nervous*."

His face softened. "It's okay. I know how you are. So, ghostbusters, huh?"

She smiled a big smile. "Yes. *Official* ghostbusters."

Pekin fretted as she and Scout entered the Cracker Barrel

Restaurant. She'd felt compelled to bring up the fact that they were running late more than once. Scout rolled his eyes as he followed her in.

She spotted a severe-looking woman in a somber black business suit and walked in that direction, but Scout grabbed her arm and indicated a geometric print-wearing woman smiling and waving at them. Pekin took one last look at the somber woman, then followed Scout to the table with their apparent client. She couldn't help feeling the plump cheery person was quite different from what she expected the owner of a haunted house to look like.

"Hello, dears," the woman said. "You must be the investigators?"

"Yes, Ms., um, Collins. We're pleased to meet you."

The three of them stared at each other awkwardly for a moment before the woman waved at the table and said, "Why don't we all sit down."

"I was intrigued by your letter," Pekin said in her most grown up voice. "How can we help you?" She remembered Scout was with her and said, "This is my partner, Scout. He'll be assisting on the assignment if you decide to work with us. Oh, and I'm Pekin. Pekin Dewlap."

"Pleased to meet you both," the Pucci-clad woman said, her cheerful manner turning all business. "I wonder, have you any experience?"

Pekin flushed red. "Well, uh, this will be our first case, actually."

The woman narrowed her eyes.

Before she could speak, Pekin hurried on. "But I know we can do a great job for you." She cleared her throat. "I used to see ghosts. I saw ghosts all the time when I was younger. I've been so busy with school the last couple of years that I admit I've tried to avoid them."

"Ms. Collins, I can attest that Pekin is very focused and driven. One might almost say obsessed."

Pekin poked him with her elbow and glowered at him.

He coughed. "What I mean is, Pekin takes this very seriously and will do a great job for you."

Ms. Collins looked from one to the other, her thumb and index finger cradling her chin.

"What, exactly, would you need us to do for you?" Pekin asked, taking her laptop from her bag and opening the document with her talking points.

"Well, you see, the Elmwood property has been in our family for generations. My great, great grandfather built the house. It was magnificent in its day, believe you me. Unfortunately, the years, and negligent family members, have contributed to its current state. I hadn't been in the house at all for many years, but feel it's time to do something with it. Either sell it or find a tenant. It's been very costly to maintain vacant for all this time."

"It does seem, um, somewhat worn out," Pekin offered.

"You haven't said what this is all about," Scout said, adopting what Pekin thought was a business tone.

Elonia patted her hair, a bouffant reminiscent of the 60s. "No one's lived in Elmwood for many years. Now, perhaps, it's time to reclaim it. It's been uninhabited for decades. It was passed down to me quite a long time ago, and I've dutifully maintained it. Kept it, I mean. I haven't really had the inclination to do anything with it. I must admit I'm tired of hanging on to it given its present circumstances."

"What about getting a heavy-duty cleaning company? And some paint?"

"Miss Dewlap, I'm afraid the problems with the house run a little deeper than mere dirt."

"I'm sorry, Ms. Collins. Please continue."

Stupid, Dewlap, she thought. *You don't want to alienate the client before you're even hired.*

"Thank you. I'll be blunt. There's something in that house that prevents any attempts to take it back."

"Something?" Scout said. "What kind of something?"

Elonia straightened her shoulders and in a determined voice said, "I believe it's a ghost...or a poltergeist."

"I don't think it could be a poltergeist," Pekin interjected. "Poltergeists are manifestations of someone, often a teenage girl, who actually lives in the house. By manifestation, I mean the living person's energy, be it anger, resentment, whatever, actually causes destruction. In contrast, a ghost is a dead person. Of course, there are varying opinions on this theory, and I suppose it's possible that a poltergeist could be a ghost." A sense of pride flowed through Pekin as she demonstrated her knowledge of the supernatural.

"Yes, well, be that as it may, there's something in that house."

"Please tell us about the *something*, Ms. Collins." Scout sounded like an investigative reporter. Pekin could kiss him for stepping up.

"Yeah, do you see anything, or do things move around, or what?" Pekin was typing busily, frowning as she chided herself for using *yeah* instead of *yes*.

"It's, perhaps, intangible. But it's there. When you enter the house it's as if a weight settles on you and dread creeps into your bones."

Pekin shivered and glanced at Scout, who seemed to be hanging on Elonia's words.

"Did these...uh...odd sensations happen recently?" Pekin asked, fingers poised over the keyboard.

"Oh, no. In fact, until I decided to visit Elmwood, to evaluate what it would take to make the house habitable, no one had lived there for decades."

"Why's that?" Scout asked.

"Because it's not safe," Elonia said. "Whatever is in that house, I feel, is sinister. It doesn't want anyone there." She smoothed her dress, perhaps desiring a chance to assemble the facts she needed to share. "A distant cousin attempted to move in back in the 70s. They didn't stay long. In fact, they didn't stay at all. Perhaps because they were embarrassed or, more probably, they didn't feel anyone would believe them, very little is known about their history with Elmwood. But my cousin, Gregory Cahill, is said to have heard noises in the walls, and once he fell down the stairs, insisting he'd been pushed. And, before the Cahills, there'd been that tragedy where the child of the family who lived at Elmwood in the early part of the century vanished from the home. She was never seen again. Before Gregory attempted to live in it, the house had sat empty since the events of 1918."

"Wait. There was a tragedy?" Scout asked.

"Yes. Until the tragedy, I've heard, it had always been a happy place. I understand lots of grand entertaining was carried on, until Miranda disappeared.

"What was Miranda's last name?" Pekin asked as she furiously typed.

"Talbert. Miranda Talbert. She was 14 when she went missing. No one was ever arrested for the crime. It was big news in the early part of the century."

"I believe this could very well be what's behind the activity you've described happening in the house," Pekin said. "It makes sense. Miranda's ghost is angry because she was never avenged."

"I've thought that it might be Miranda. I suppose you could be correct. Now then, when can you start?"

"I searched online to see what information I could find about your house," Pekin said. "I didn't find anything about a missing person."

"Well, you didn't know her name. I don't believe the stories would revolve around the address of the *house* back then. A search for "Miranda Talbert" might provide information."

"What's in the house now?" Scout asked. "Is it empty?"

"No. Miranda's parents lived in that house until they both passed on. All their furniture is still in the house."

"Why didn't anyone take it? Wasn't it pretty nice stuff?" Scout asked.

"Oh, it was. But the house was unwelcoming to anyone who entered it. Threatening somehow. No one was brave enough to disturb whatever walked those empty halls."

Pekin tried to hide the shiver that ran through her body.

"But holding onto a big house for so long doesn't make sense. Someone had to be paying the bills for it."

"The Talberts created a trust for the house to maintain it. In case Miranda came home someday. They were a wealthy family. But, it's been a hundred years, and the funds of the trust are running out. Obviously, Miranda won't be coming home again."

"Interesting. What would you want us to do, Ms. Collins?" Scout asked.

"Why, make the ghost go away, of course. I need you to rid the house of Miranda."

Pekin was both excited and leery. She liked the idea of having a client, but it suddenly hit her that she would have to deal with an actual ghost. Apparently, a ghost who didn't like visitors. From the comfort of her bedroom, it hadn't seemed such a scary proposition. Seeing ghosts in the past was one thing, an encounter with a potentially violent entity was on a whole different level.

Elonia peered at her. It made Pekin nervous, but she pasted what she hoped was a brave smile on her face and said, "I believe we can help you with that. Right, Scout?"

Scout didn't answer right away until Pekin nudged him. "Uh, sure."

Pekin scowled at his slow response.

"I mean, I'm sure we can handle this. What happens next?" he said.

The older woman put a finger to her lips in contemplation. "You're awfully young, though."

"Oh," Pekin said, her smile fading. "We *are* still in high school, but we'll work very hard. I promise. And remember, I do have firsthand experience with ghosts. Are you speaking with other ghost removal companies?"

"No. No, I'm not. In fact, you're the first ghost removal company I've heard of. So—"

Elonia took a deep breath and reached in her Coach bag. She withdrew an old key and placed it on the table in front of her, then slid it over to Pekin. "This will get you inside. It's number 12. I would suggest you not go at night."

"No worries about that," Scout said.

Elonia smiled for the first time since they sat down. "You haven't mentioned your fee."

"Let us write up a work order and we'll email it to you," Pekin responded.

"Thank you. I will arrange to have all the utilities turned on in the house."

"Great. I suppose it would help if we could see once we get inside," Pekin said.

"Yes. It would."

With that, the three of them stood and said their goodbyes, and Elonia left the restaurant. Pekin started to follow, but Scout said, "Yeah. What are we charging for this?"

Pekin looked sheepish. "I don't have any idea. What do you think? Should we charge a flat fee or charge by the hour?"

"Well, we don't have any idea how much time this is all going to take. Maybe we need to do it by the hour so that we get some idea—"

"Of what to charge the *next* client?" Pekin asked helpfully.

"Yeah, sure. What to charge the next client. Let's take care of this one first, okay?"

"You…you sound like you're going to help me with this. I was worried I was going to have to do it alone. I mean, Amber and I were going to go it alone. Are you in?" She hoped he didn't see the flush creeping over her cheeks. Scout *had* to be there with her. She wouldn't be able to bear the disappointment if he wasn't. Because, if she was being honest, another reason she was so insistent on this ghost company was because it would mean time spent with Scout. Lots of time. She snuck a look at him, and found him staring at her.

He reached over and touched her cheek. "Why are you blushing?"

She was horrified. "I'm *not* blushing. It's…it's hot in here. That's all."

"Why not," he said with a smile that showed off his dimples. "It might be fun to hang out in a haunted house. I think we should go at midnight."

"Absolutely *not*. I only want to see ghosts in the daylight. I can't wait 'til we tell Amber everything."

"I can imagine how pleased she's going to be with this development," Scout said, with a laugh.

"Are *you* pleased, Scout?" She looked at him, shy all of a sudden.

He shrugged. When he saw a look of disappointment cross her face, he said, "Anything for you, Pekie. Sure. I'm pleased."

"Because of the ghosts or because of me?" *Had she really said that out loud?*

He smiled and put his arm around her shoulders. "You, Pekie. Always you."

She laughed shakily. "That's what I thought. You just want to spend time with me."

He laughed. "Are you flirting with me?"

"*Moi*? I thought you were flirting with *me*." She turned toward the door. "Come on. Let's get out of here." She walked ahead, glad he couldn't see her face, where the blush was growing deeper. *I can't believe I said that to him.* "Do you think Amber is going to freak?"

He moved ahead and held the door open for her. His eyes scanned her face and he looked like he was going to comment, but must have decided to keep it to himself.

She forced herself to meet his eyes.

"Maybe. Just a little," he said. "But you can talk her into it. I've seen you do it."

"I know. I'm almost afraid to tell her, especially since it's not a happy ghost."

Chapter Seven

AMBER, PEKIN, AND SCOUT sat on the deck behind Amber's house. It was a pleasant Sunday afternoon, and the Adirondack chairs were arranged facing each other around a low table that held bottles of water and cans of Pepsi in a bucket of ice. Scout's long legs were stretched out in front of him, and he leaned back, his hands behind his head as he listened to the conversation. He let Pekin do all the talking, watching her babble on.

"I was worried she wouldn't hire us, because we're still in school, but we managed to convince her. Cool, huh?" Pekin said. She pulled the key out of the pocket of her shorts and held it out for Amber to see. "I love this old key. It's so...so...*cool.*"

Amber barely glanced at the key. She was as pleased as Pekin had imagined she'd be. Or, in layman's terms, not at all.

"I really don't like ghosts, Pekin. I really don't."

"Aren't you excited that we have our first customer? She will *pay* us."

"Not enough. And I don't want some ghost to scare the bejeezus out of me."

"Scout will be there. He won't let anything happen to us."

"Yeah, like he has a ton of experience with haunted houses."

"She's got a point there," Scout piped in.

"Look, we're going to go in the daytime. We won't be there after dark when it would be really creepy. I think we should go next Saturday. I don't want to do it after school, because we wouldn't have enough time. I mean, I don't know how long it will take to get the presence to leave the house."

"Or how we will actually *get* the presence to go," Scout said.

Chapter Eight

S ATURDAY MORNING, SCOUT PULLED up to the curb of 12 Elmwood. The teens climbed out and stood on the sidewalk staring up at the hulking structure. Pekin, the only one who'd seen the house in person, led the way up to the front door. Amber looked around, scrunching up her face to show her distaste.

The house must once have been magnificent. A red brick colonial, two steps led up to a porch with a red door, its paint faded and peeling. On each side of the door was a white column, also faded and peeling. And grimy. There was a sagging porch overhang supported by the two columns.

Pekin produced the old key and, taking a deep breath, slipped it into the rusty lock. At first there was resistance as she turned the key back and forth. Scout moved her aside and added that *guy* thing that makes unruly mechanical items respond.

"Wa la," he said, puffing out his chest as he pushed open the squeaky door.

"I don't think *wa la* is a real term," she said, but quickly added "never mind" when Scout rolled his eyes.

He stepped aside with a mock bow to usher Pekin into the house. She peeked over the threshold. It was dim and dusty inside. For a moment, she felt reluctance over entering any further. But her reputation was on the line. She stood straighter and bravely stepped into the murky interior. "Come on, you guys. It's all good."

"I don't think it's so good," Amber said, once she'd sidled up to Pekin.

Scout waved his hand in front of his face. "It smells like a house that hasn't seen a human in 50 years." He walked into the room to the right and pushed aside the heavy drapes covering one of the tall windows along the front of the house. Before he could say "now we can see," they covered their noses and mouths, coughing and sneezing as decades of dust billowed out of the threadbare curtains, and tumbled back out the front door so they could breathe fresh air.

Pekin punched Scout in the arm.

"Oww," he said, rubbing the spot. "It was dark in there."

Pekin rubbed his arm and apologized. "Sorry, Scout. We're all on edge. I freaked out. You did the right thing, and we should open more of them. Sure wish we had facemasks or bandanas or something."

"We can hold our breath each time."

"Or, we can wait outside and Scout can come get us when they're all open," Amber said.

"That's not very nice for Scout."

"It's okay. I can hold my breath and step outside after each one to let the dust settle."

"Thanks, Scout," Pekin said. A wave of happiness washed over her, noticing he seemed into the adventure. She hoped Amber would get on board, too.

Once Scout gave the all clear, Pekin and Amber reentered the foyer. It was brighter, but not as much as Pekin had hoped. The drapes were open, but the dirt and grime of decades still coated the windows. Scout was gray from top to bottom. He had about fifty years' worth of dust clinging to every part of his body.

"Come back outside," Pekin said as she whacked him several times, her hand covering her mouth and nose to protect her from the cloud of dust rising into the air around him, reminding her of Pig-Pen from the Peanuts cartoons. She peered at him closely. "Stand still." Taking a tissue from her pocket, she wiped away the dust that clung to his eyelashes.

"Thanks," he said with a charming smile. Heat burned her cheeks, and she looked away.

Hands on hips, Pekin surveyed the grand foyer. An ornate cherrywood staircase rose to her left. In her imagination she could see ladies in beautiful ball gowns grandly descending the stairs, gloved hands on the banister. Straight ahead, the foyer continued as a hallway. There were four doorways opening to the right and one to the left, with the hallway ending in a service porch of some kind. To her right, she noticed dust motes floating in the light coming in through the windows. Ghostly forms under dingy sheets were formed by furniture the Talberts left behind. Pekin couldn't wait to start uncovering all of it.

As she reached out a hand with the intention of lifting the closest sheet, Scout stopped her.

"If you thought the dust on the drapes was bad, these furniture covers will be even worse. We really should get some facemasks before we start that. Do you want me to go pick some up? I can be back in half an hour."

"No!" Amber said. "You can't leave me in this haunted house alone with Pekin. She promised you'd take care of us."

Pekin glared at her. "Thanks a lot."

Amber's cheeks flushed. "I mean, let me go. I'm sure the two of you can accomplish more than I can." She looked pointedly at Scout. "And I won't stay a *minute* in this house if you're not here, too."

"Good grief, Amber," Pekin said. "Besides, you only got your license a month ago. Scout doesn't want you driving his car."

"No problem," Scout said, handing Amber his keys. "Just be careful. I don't need any more dents. If you think of anything else you think we might need, go for it."

Amber didn't need to be told twice. Her hand was on the doorknob when she turned back. "Either of you guys have any money? I only have a five on me."

"Um—" Pekin said.

"Here." Scout pulled his wallet out of his back pocket and handed her two twenties.

"Thanks." She grabbed the money and was out the door in a flash.

"This is your thing, Pekin, not Amber's," Scout said. "I think she hates it."

Pekin hung her head. "You're right, but I want you guys to be part of it. Do you think I'm wrong?"

"I don't necessarily think you're wrong. Still, you can't blame Amber for the way she feels. You should give her a break."

"I'll try. I mean, I'll try not to get irritated with her, but I'm not quite ready to let her resign."

Pekin stepped outside and sat down on the front porch. "Thanks, by the way. For giving Amber money. I should have thought of that."

"Give yourself a break. It's your first haunted house. How could you know what you…we…were getting into?"

"I know, but—"

"No buts. Think of this as a learning experience."

"I suppose."

Scout sat down beside her, put his arm around her shoulders, and gave her a hug. Her breath caught in her throat. That's all she needed, for him to notice that she got all weird when he was close to her. She shrugged and he took his arm way. *That* wasn't what she wanted him to do. Besides, it was more of a shiver than a shrug.

"Thanks, Scout. You know, for everything." She looked up at him and he put his big hand on top of her head and ruffled her hair.

"Oh! My ponytail!" Her hands flew up to adjust the elastic band holding her hair back. He laughed and stood up.

"Sorry. Didn't mean to ruin your hairdo."

"I don't have a hairdo. I have a ponytail and I—" She huffed and stood as well. "It's okay. It just surprised me. You can touch my hair whenever you want to." *Ack! Had she really said that out loud? What was with her mouth saying whatever it wanted!*

He studied her. This time she did blush.

"Who knows? I might want to do that," he said with a grin. He ruffled her hair again. "You don't have to be embarrassed. You look cute."

She felt her cheeks redden for the umpteenth time.

"You don't have to blush every time I say something to you."

"I'm not blushing! It's hot out. I'm glad I wore shorts."

"Me, too."

Pekin wasn't sure if he meant he was glad he wore shorts, or that *she* wore shorts.

"But I suppose, looking at how dirty this house is, we should have worn jeans."

"Or coveralls," Scout said.

"Or real *Ghostbusters* jumpsuits."

Scout laughed and shook his head.

"I guess we should wait for Amber to get back with the masks, but I'm dying to start exploring," Pekin said. "I bet this was some showplace in its day."

"Yeah, but—"

"I know. You think we should wait." She looked over her shoulder through the open door at the dim interior of the old estate. Suddenly, she jumped to her feet. "Hey, we should name this place *Elmwood Manor*. What do you think?"

He rolled his eyes. "Whatever you say. Apparently, you're the boss of us."

"Thank you for acknowledging that. I'm the boss and I christen this place *Elmwood Manor*."

"Pekin, I'm getting worried about you. This is just a job."

"But—"

"But nothing. Don't get carried away. That's all I'm saying." Scout clambered to his feet. "I wish we had some water. I hope Amber gets back soon." He stepped off the porch to scan the street for any sign of her.

Pekin watched him for a moment, then turned her attention to the front of the house, noticing the cockeyed "12" by the door. She tried to push the "2" back into an upright position, but without a hammer and nails, there was nothing to hold it up, and it swung loosely back upside down when she let it go.

"Here she comes," Scout said pulling Pekin's attention from the upside down 2.

Amber arrived on the porch with her purchases, handing the plastic bag to Pekin.

Pekin passed out the masks and stuffed the plastic bag in her backpack. With the mask secured in place, she rubbed her hands together. "Here we go," she said, her voice muffled, her eyes growing big with excitement.

She stepped into the front room, then stopped. "We really should have brought some large garbage bags for the old sheets." She surveyed the room. "Never mind, we can stack them up and deal with them later."

"Hello!"

They all turned toward the open front door.

"I wanted to stop by and see how...what—" Elonia Collins stopped talking as she looked past them into the room.

"Ms. Collins!" Pekin said, surprised. She hurriedly pulled off her mask. She extended her hand but noticed how dirty it looked and wiped it on her shorts.

Elonia smiled as she took Pekin's hand.

"You remember Scout, of course," Pekin said. "This is Amber, part of our team. She wasn't able to meet you before.

"Pleased to meet you, Amber," Elonia said with a nod as she stepped into the parlor.

"You, too," Amber mumbled, staring at the older woman's head, seemingly awed by the bouffant hairdo.

"Be careful," Pekin said to her. "It's kind of a mess in here." She couldn't help noticing the brightly colored geometric patterned silk blouse the older woman wore with fire engine red slacks.

"It certainly is." Elonia sneezed at the dust.

"Um, we thought we'd need to clean up some before we try to contact Miranda. There's a lot of dust on everything."

"I noticed." Elonia cradled her chin with her thumb and index finder as she surveyed the covered furniture and dirty windows. "I don't want to keep you from your *process*," she said, turning toward the door. Then she hesitated. "Please feel free to add any expenses you incur to your bill," she said before turning back and leaving.

"That was odd," Amber said.

"It was, kind of," Pekin responded. "I mean, was she even here a whole minute?" She knew the real reason Elonia had left quickly was because she didn't want to encounter Miranda. Of course, Pekin wasn't going to say that in front of Amber.

"Well, let's get to it." Pekin approached a large covered object and lifted an edge of the old sheet. She jerked the sheet and it slid off, releasing a cloud of dust that, even with a facemask, wasn't pleasant to breathe. She waved her hand in front of her face. "Ugh. I think we need gasmasks."

"Maybe you should remove them more carefully," Amber offered.

The newly revealed object was a grand piano. It must have been grand at one time. At the moment it was covered with a fine layer of dust that had managed to sift through the sheet. Pekin lifted the cover from the keys and plunked a few of them. "Could really use tuning," she said. "If I'd ever taken piano lessons as a child, I bet I'd really appreciate this."

"Why do we have to uncover all this furniture anyway?" Amber asked.

"Aren't you curious?"

"Not really."

"We don't *have* to take the covers off, but this way it gives us a way to familiarize ourselves with Elmwood Manor."

Amber opened her mouth to speak, but Scout interjected, "Just go with it."

"Okay."

"We might as well explore a little, since we don't know how long it's going to take the ghost to show itself," Scout said.

"Her name is Miranda," Pekin said. "If Elmwood Manor is haunted, it's probably Miranda wandering the halls."

After uncovering the rest of the furniture in the sitting room, Pekin decided it was enough. "Let's walk through the rest of the rooms and see what we can see."

"We're not going to clean the whole house, are we?" Amber whined with a frown.

"No. This is mostly for our benefit. If we're going to hang out here, I think it's more pleasant if it's at least a little cleaner. Besides, we can barely see through the windows. Even during the day, it's dark in here. We should wash a few windows."

"If you say so," said a still unhappy Amber.

They moved from the sitting room to the library on the opposite side of the entry hall, admiring the dusty row upon row of books and the sliding mahogany ladder for accessing the higher shelves. Past the stairway on the right were what was possibly an office and a large formal dining room, and then the kitchen.

"Wow." Amber stood in the center of the kitchen, taking it all in. "This room is massive!" In the center was a large tiled island. Dirty windows above the porcelain sinks would have given a view into the overgrown backyard. A large wooden trestle table sat along one wall, with a bench running along the front. No sheet covered it, and the layer of dust was thick enough it might have cushioned anything that dropped on the table.

Off the kitchen at the back of the house was a mudroom. Grimy pegs hung on the wall opposite a door to the outside. Scout tried the door, but it was locked, and its window was so dirty that even trying to rub a clear spot in the dirt didn't give much of a view into the backyard. He shrugged and followed Pekin as she wandered back to the foyer.

The second Pekin put a foot on the bottom step of the staircase, Amber whined, "I'm not going up there."

"Fine, you can wait for us down here. Scout and I will go up."

"You can't leave me by myself!" Pekin could tell Amber was verging on panic. Her picking at her perfectly manicured nails was a dead giveaway.

"Then you have to come with us. How are we going to explore the house if we don't go upstairs? Stop worrying. We'll stick close together. Nothing is going to happen."

"You don't know that," Amber muttered under her breath, following Pekin and Scout up the stairs.

They counted four bedrooms and three bathrooms on the second level. Claw-foot bathtubs and sinks with porcelain knobs gave a certain charm to each of the bathrooms. The charm was lessened by the grime covering every surface.

Heavy, dusty draperies hung at the windows of the bedrooms, casting a shadowy dimness over the rooms. No one wanted to get close enough to touch them, out of fear there would be a repeat of Scout's original attempt to open the first-floor drapes. Some of the bureau drawers were partially open. A closer look showed the drawers to be empty.

"I wonder which room was Miranda's," Pekin mused.

"No clue," Scout said.

"Still," Pekin said. "The largest room at the front of the house was probably the master. I think a younger girl like Miranda would want…." She tapped her chin with her forefinger, scanning the hallway for a moment. She wandered down the hall, poking her head in each door. "This one," she said matter-of-factly of the room at the back overlooking the yard. "I think she would have picked this one."

"Why do we care which room was hers?" Amber asked.

"Because. I don't know. I just want to try to get a feel for her. Maybe this is where she hangs out." Pekin walked into the room and looked around. There was a canopy bed with a carved wooden frame that was probably white. The bedcovers remaining were threadbare and filthy. A dresser and small desk graced opposite walls. Pekin examined each carefully, opening and closing drawers, hoping for a scrap of something, anything, that might be meaningful.

A closet door on one wall was not quite closed. Pekin opened it, flashing her light around the small space. It was dusty and empty, at least that's how it seemed at first. As she started to close the door, her flashlight beam fell on something in the corner, and she leaned down to see what it was.

"Did you find something?" Scout asked, crossing to the closet.

"I think it's a doll."

"Can I see?" Amber said.

Pekin backed out of the closet to give her friends a view of the small lump in the corner. Scout bent down and lifted it by an arm, then brought it out, attempting to brush cobwebs off the doll's face.

Amber leaned in for a better look. "Eww. Get it away."

"Let me see," Pekin said, reaching to take the doll from Scout. She handled it gingerly, both because it was old and because it was very dirty. Grime and dust bunnies, and sticky cobwebs, covered its white cotton dress. Pekin tapped her fingernail against its face. "Porcelain, I think."

The doll's eyes stared blankly at Pekin, the layers of dust disguising their true color. She licked her finger and smudged it over the doll's cheek, exposing a pink tint. Its lips were cherry red. "She'd be very pretty when she's cleaned up," Pekin said.

"What are you going to do with her?" Amber asked.

"I suppose I'll leave her where I found her. If she was Miranda's, maybe Miranda loves her. I wonder if she knows it's in there." She placed the doll back in the corner of the closet and closed the door. "Let's go. More to see."

Chapter Nine

H ALFWAY DOWN THE HALL, Pekin noticed a stairway leading up to a single door at the top of the next landing. It was narrower and ricketier than the main staircase. "We have to go up there."

Amber stamped her foot, disturbing layers of dust. "No! This house is dirty and ugly and I hate it. I won't go into another scary room."

Scout looked skeptically up the stairs. "I don't particularly want to go up there either."

"You guys, it's part of the job. What if that room is where Miranda hangs out?"

"Hence, I don't want to go to that scary room." Amber crossed her arms and pressed her glossed lips into a tight line.

"Look, it's still daylight. Let's quickly poke our heads in and look around. Then we can mark it off our list." She put her hand on Amber's arm. "Please."

Amber glared in exasperation. "Okay, fine. But remember you said we'll be really quick."

Pekin started up the steps, worried the door would be locked. *Wouldn't that be just peachy?* But other than creaking a little, the doorknob turned and the door squeaked opened. Pekin stuck her head in. The interior was dim, light from the sole window doing little to relieve the gloom.

"We need more flashlights. I brought an extra one just in case."

"I brought one, too," Scout added. "It's downstairs in my backpack."

"Mine, too. Wait here and I'll go get them." She noticed Amber's expression and pulled the door closed. "There. You'll be safe until I get back."

Pekin returned and handed a flashlight to Amber and one to Scout and reopened the door. She took a deep breath and turned on her light.

"Okay, here we go," she said in a feeble attempt not to sound like she was whistling past a graveyard.

"Why are you making me do this?" Amber scrunched her shoulders as if to make herself as small as possible. She shined her flashlight around the dark room and screeched when her beam fell on a scowling face.

"Quit complaining. We have work to do," said the face in question.

"But...what if we find something?"

"That's the point, silly."

The third-floor room's only window was opposite the door. Pekin's flashlight picked out mist-shrouded forms as she made her way to the window. A cold chill ran down her spine as she remembered seeing something in that window when Campbell drove her past 12 Elmwood. She *thought* she had seen something. She peered out the window, then stepped back and stared at her reflection in the window, holding her breath, preparing to run if a scary, ghostly shape appeared in the glass behind her, *á la* a million haunted house movies. When nothing happened, she allowed herself to breathe again and swung her flashlight back into the room.

Near the window, the beam fell on a crib. Pekin softly touched the faded bouquet of roses painted on its side. Maybe it wasn't faded after all. Maybe if the layers of dust were removed....

A high-pitched shriek pulled her from her thoughts. "There's someone there!" Amber cried, pointing a shaky finger toward a corner of the attic. Scout shone his light in the direction she indicated and all of them jumped. A human figure hovered in the gloom.

"Scout," Amber whispered, huddling behind him and peeking around him at the spectre.

Closer examination showed it to be an old dress form, with a large hat perched on top. It looked a little too human in the dimly lit room.

"Can't we go now?" Amber whimpered.

"It's just a mannequin," Pekin said. "I'm not done yet, but I'll hurry."

Scout put his arm around Amber's shoulders. "We can explore

together. You're safe with me."

Amber looked up at him, a trembling smile on her face. "Thank you, Scout. At least *you* care whether something bad happens to me."

"Good grief," Pekin muttered.

Amber stayed close to Scout as they moved around the room, their flashlights scanning side to side. Scout's beam fell on an old cedar chest. "Hey, Pekin. Check this out."

Pekin's foot kicked a small red ball with dirty white stars which skittered off across the floor. She looked after it as she knelt down and tried without luck to open the lid of the cedar chest. Scout gave it a go as well, but the chest was locked.

"Should we break it open?" he asked.

"Let's wait. Maybe we'll find the key somewhere. I don't want to ruin it."

The hairs on the back of Pekin's neck stood up. She had the oddest sensation of being watched, and looked over her shoulder to scan the room. "Do you guys—" she started but stopped when it appeared they hadn't noticed.

"Can we go now?" Amber asked again.

Pekin gave a nod, standing up and shining her flashlight around the attic one last time. "Yeah. Let's get out of here."

After closing the attic door, the three of them tromped back down to the second floor.

The sound of a door slamming caused Amber to squeal. They all looked at each other.

"Do you think that was downstairs?" Pekin asked.

"No. It sounded like it was on this floor," Scout said.

"There's no one in this house but us," Amber said, her voice shaky, her eyes big. She looked to be on the verge of either fleeing or peeing her pants. Pekin couldn't tell which.

Pekin stared down the hallway. The door to Miranda's room was closed. She took a tentative step in that direction.

"What are you doing?" Amber shrieked. "We have to get out of here!"

"I think Amber's right, Pekin," Scout said in a voice considerably quieter than Amber's.

"I need to see what closed that door," she responded, trying to sound braver than she felt. "You don't have to go with me. Wait here."

Without giving them a chance to argue, Pekin headed down the hallway. She gulped before grabbing hold of the doorknob. It turned, but the door didn't open. Pekin pushed on the door, and jammed her shoulder into it, but it wouldn't budge. Before she could take her hand off the knob, the house seemed to shudder and moan. She slowly backed away, then turned and ran back to her friends, and they all flew down the stairs.

Amid the rumbling noises, Pekin heard an eerie *Get out*, but she was sure it was her imagination.

Chapter Ten

Scout held the front door open until everyone was out. As he stepped across the threshold, the door slammed with such force, it knocked him off his feet. He landed on all fours but turned over and scooted backwards amid the shrieks of Pekin and Amber.

Scrambling to his feet, followed by the girls, he ran for his car. His shaky hand made it difficult to unlock the car, until he used both hands to steady the key.

The Corolla tore away from the curb. No one spoke until they were a block away and could breathe again.

"What the hell?" Scout said.

Pekin said nothing. She looked out the car window deep in thought.

"We're not going back there," Amber said. "Ever!"

"It told us to get out," Scout added.

Pekin turned. "You guys heard that, too? I thought I imagined it."

"Oh yeah, we heard it," he said. "Whatever it was sounded pretty definite it doesn't want us there."

"Do you guys know what this means?" Pekin asked, all but jumping up and down in her seat with excitement. "The house is actually *haunted*. We really have our work cut out for us."

"Holy crap! What are you talking about? We're done." Scout stared at her like she'd lost her mind.

"We are *not* done. We have a job to do."

"Aren't you freaked out by that house?" Amber asked.

"I'm trying not to be. I really want this to work. Do you guys know how great it would be to succeed at this?"

"There's a real ghost in that house. I don't *like* ghosts. I *hate* them," Amber said, poking Pekin with a vibrant orange-painted nail.

"I need to think about this. Please don't make up your minds until we've had time to think. It's an *adventure*. Aren't you excited about that?"

"I'm kind of leaning with Amber on this, but we can talk tomorrow."

"DON'T YOU THINK WE'RE GETTING a little old for make-believe?" Scout said as he set his lunch down on their cafeteria table. "It's almost the end of the year. It's going to be busy between now and then. I'm not sure—"

"Scout, how can you call it make-believe after we all heard that scary voice?" Pekin's voice was catching and tears were threatening. "I can't believe you'd back out now. I know this is more my thing than yours...or Amber's...but I never would have started all this if I thought you wouldn't be with me."

"You started it way before you talked to us about it. You ordered business cards and scared up a haunted house. Why do you even need us?"

"Because I do." She turned her head so he wouldn't see the tears that had escaped, and tried to wipe them away. She felt his hand on her shoulder and looked at him. "You're right. I did it all wrong. I thought...I thought this would be like it always is, and the three of us would be in it together. I don't want to have to do it alone." She dipped her head. "What should I do, Scout, call Elonia and tell her I'm sorry but we can't help her?"

Before he could answer, Amber dropped her tray and sat down next to Pekin. "What's up, you guys?"

When no one answered, Amber looked from one friend to the other. "What'd I miss? Is something going on between you guys?"

Pekin was horrified. Blushing, she picked up her untouched lunch and hurried away.

"What did I say?" Pekin heard Amber ask Scout, but she didn't stop.

She dumped her untouched tacos in the trashcan and headed to the library. A good place to hide out while she thought about the situation and got herself under control. Maybe she *would* have to back out of the Elmwood deal.

More than that, she'd overreacted to Amber's question about whether something was going on between her and Scout. She knew Amber hadn't meant it that way. Of course Amber didn't think there was something going on. Because there wasn't. Scout didn't look at her as anything but a friend.

She felt numb, unsure what would happen next, and spent the rest of her lunch hour with her hand propping up her chin, staring into space.

AMBER CAUGHT UP WITH PEKIN BETWEEN CLASSES. "Scout told me you're upset with us."

Pekin pretended to look for a book in her locker. "It's okay. I know neither of you wants to do Elmwood with me. I can handle it by myself." She straightened and slammed her locker shut. "Don't worry about it." She couldn't help that tears were gathering in her eyes, but she didn't want Amber to see, so she slung her backpack over her shoulder, her face turned.

Before she could walk away, Amber put her hand on Pekin's shoulder. "We've decided to stay in."

Pekin took a step before Amber's words registered. "What?"

"I said, you don't have to do it alone. We started this with you and we'll finish it."

Pekin grabbed Amber in a hug. "Oh, thank you!"

Amber watched her for a moment. "I can't say I *love* being a part of your haunted house company."

"But—"

"But Scout and I won't abandon you."

AFTER SCHOOL, PEKIN RACED UP THE STAIRS to her room. She dropped her backpack on the floor with a thud, startling the little gray and white cat, who now stretched and yawned. Pekin lay down beside Griselda and curled into a fetal position around her, burying her face in the cat's soft fur, comforted by the loud purrs.

"Am I an awful friend, Griselda?" Pekin rolled onto her back and scratched the cat's ears. "I *knew* they didn't really want to do this, but I pushed ahead and pretty much demanded they show up. Then I pouted when they weren't happy about it. *Now,* they've caved and said they'd still be in because they don't want to let me down. But I guess I let them down." She started to cry.

"What do I do now? We took the job. Do we stop so I can let them off the hook? Oh, Griselda. Am I a bad person?"

Her phone vibrated with a text from Amber. *You okay?*

She picked up her phone and looked at the message. *I'm really sorry,* she texted back.

Apology accepted. Everything will work out.

Promise?

Are you okay?

Pekin sighed. Now her friends were worried. She sat up straighter and texted *I'm fine. Don't worry about me, okay?*

Okay. See you at school tomorrow.

AT LUNCHTIME, PEKIN AND AMBER sat side by side on a shady bench in the quad waiting for an unusually late Scout. "What's keeping him?" Pekin asked.

Scanning the courtyard that teemed with students on their lunch break, she spotted him. Talking to Vanessa Dooley. Tall, *beautiful* Vanessa Dooley.

Amber followed her gaze then glanced back at Pekin noticing the glare Pekin was directing toward Vanessa.

"Are you jealous?"

When Pekin turned to her, the look on her face gave her away.

"You *are*," Amber said. "*You like Scout.*"

"I don't—"

"I thought I imagined those wistful looks you get when you think he's not looking."

"I don't have wistful looks," Pekin huffed, afraid she wasn't imagining that her face was turning red.

"If you say so."

Pekin was silent for a moment, feeling caught. "You can't tell him, okay? I'm sure he doesn't feel that way about me."

"How do you know?"

"Because, he's talking to Vanessa Dooley. Look at her. Look at *me*. I can't compete with her."

"You don't have to. You're smart, funny, loyal. She can't hold a candle to all you have to offer. You're making a big deal out of him talking to another girl. He spends his free time with us. With *you*. Get a grip."

"Amber, you don't...you don't...like him, too, do you?" Pekin's face reflected the sudden horror she felt at the thought that she and Amber might *both* have a crush on Scout.

"God, no. I mean, of *course* I like him. He's our best friend. But I don't *like* like him. I'm kind of into Josh Parker." She nudged Pekin with her shoulder. "Don't tell him either."

"Don't worry. Your secret's safe with me."

They were silent for a moment, then Pekin said, "He doesn't like me *that* way."

"Umm hmm. If you say so."

"Why? Do you think he does?"

Amber shrugged. "How long have you had a crush on him?"

"For a while. He changed so much since last year. He's like a *man* now." Pekin's eyes had a faraway look.

"He's a little young to be a man," Amber said. "But he's definitely hot."

"Right? He has *muscles* now. He—"

"Hey, guys." Scout dropped onto the bench beside Pekin and put an arm around her shoulders. "You okay?"

Luckily, Scout couldn't see Pekin's face as she turned to Amber and mouthed *oh my God*.

She tried for a casual response. "I wish you guys would stop asking me that. I'm *fine*. I was being bratty, okay?"

He laughed. "So, we're all good?"

"Yep," Amber said.

"I guess," Pekin said, praying her embarrassment at Scout almost overhearing her conversation with Amber didn't show.

"Cool," Scout said.

"Now that we're all sure I'm okay, you guys want to go to Benny's for breakfast Saturday?" Pekin asked. "We can talk about everything."

"Works for me," Scout said.

BENNY'S HAD BEEN THE GO-TO PLACE ever since it'd opened a few years back. It had a retro vibe, with Formica countertops and red and white checked plastic tablecloths. There was even a jukebox in the corner. It had the best burgers around and a great breakfast menu.

After coffee and hot chocolates arrived, an awkward silence hovered over their table. Amber buried her nose in her menu. Pekin did the same. Scout sipped his coffee without looking at his menu. Pekin didn't know why she and Amber bothered. They always ordered the same thing anyway.

"Okay, what do you want us to do? We don't know how to do anything," Amber said, putting down the menu. Her voice was dangerously close to being a whine.

"We could just hang out and see if anything happens. We were tired before. Maybe we didn't really hear the house tell us to get out. I mean, we were all kind of on edge, right?"

"I'm pretty sure a really creepy voice said we should get out. And the door didn't slam itself," Amber said. She shook her head. "Uh uh. I'm done."

"You said you were in," Pekin said. "Are you backing out now?"

She looked at Scout, silently asking for help. He rolled his eyes and put his hands on the table. "Come on, Amber. I'll make sure you're safe. You believe me, right?"

She looked doubtful and began picking at her nail polish. "Aren't you scared to go back there?"

"I'm a guy. I couldn't admit it even if I was," he said with a lopsided grin.

"If you promise."

"It's a go, then," Pekin said. "Hurry up and eat. We're wasting the daylight."

The mood was lighter as they left Benny's...at least until they pulled up in front of 12 Elmwood. All the chatter stopped as they looked with apprehension at the old house.

"Let's go." With forced enthusiasm, Pekin flung open her car door. Scout and Amber didn't even attempt to look eager. Amber looked doomed.

Scout slammed his car door and joined Pekin on the front walk. Amber meandered behind.

Pekin produced the old key and unlocked the door. She held her breath as she turned the knob and pushed the door open. Scout heroically stepped across the threshold first, and waved Pekin and Amber in.

Pekin pulled a handful of facemasks from the scuffed backpack she'd dropped on the floor inside the door. She bent over and retrieved several pairs of rubber gloves, then straightened up and faced her two friends.

"It's going to be okay, Amber," she said, focusing on her potential defector. "We're just going to explore a little and tidy up a bit, so we'll be more comfortable here. That's all the work we're doing on the place. I doubt that anything remotely interesting will happen."

"Yeah, but you don't know that. I was there when the house yelled at us."

"It didn't yell. We don't even know for sure that we heard something."

"I think if all three of us heard the same thing, then we do know for sure," Scout interjected.

"Who knows what it was. Maybe our imaginations got the best of us."

"You're not going to win this one, Pekin," he said. "You might as well give up."

She scowled for a second. "Let's give it a try, okay? We can spend a little time and see how it goes. If anyone gets scared, we can leave."

"Then I guess we can leave now," Amber said crossing her arms over her chest. "I'm scared."

"Wasn't it just yesterday you told me don't worry we're in? Come on, Amber. I need you guys. Don't you think it would be really cool if we could send Miranda into the light?"

Amber grabbed a facemask out of Pekin's hand. "Let's get this over with."

Pekin smiled and mouthed *Thank you* to her friend. Then she handed Scout a mask and gave each of them a set of rubber gloves.

"The parlor's done. The room next to it is a study of some sort. Let's start in there." She secured her facemask in place and marched into the room full of dusty, sheet-covered lumps. Pekin looked around to make sure all masks were on, then gingerly lifted a corner of the sheet covering the largest piece of furniture. She began folding back the covering, careful to disturb as little dust as possible.

When the sheet was lying in a pile on the floor, Pekin's eyes lit up. "Look, you guys. It's a rolltop desk. Who knows what we might find in it."

"Should all of us ooh and ahh over the desk, or do you want us to actually accomplish something?" Scout asked. Pekin thought it was mean, but refused to let it get her down.

"I'll look through the desk. You guys pick a shroud and see what's under it."

"I'd appreciate it if you didn't refer to the sheets as shrouds," Amber grumbled.

Pekin shook her head. "Whatever."

As she opened the top of the desk, something bounced off and onto the floor.

Scout and Amber turned in time to see what looked like a nickel roll across the floor. Pekin followed the coin as it rolled out the door of the study and made a sharp left turn and then a right before it bumped into the bottom step of the staircase and fell over. She gulped. The coin seemed to have a deliberate destination in mind. She hoped her friends hadn't noticed, but when she looked over her shoulder she saw two faces looking back.

"What the—" Scout sputtered.

"We didn't just see that, did we?" Pekin bent and picked up the coin, an old buffalo head nickel.

"Don't touch it," Amber hissed.

Pekin gave a nervous laugh, pulled a tissue out of her pocket, then rubbed the nickel. She held it up for her friends to see. "It's okay,

Amber. It's just a nickel. 1918. That's *really* old. Like over a hundred years. It's so cool."

Amber watched from a distance as Scout took it out of Pekin's hand and examined it. "I wonder how much it's worth."

Pekin took it back. "We're not selling it. First, it's not ours. And second...well, I don't know what second is, but I'm sure there is one." She gave a cautious look up the stairs, and headed back into the study.

"I didn't like that," Amber said.

Pekin didn't have to ask what she meant. "Oh, don't worry about it. It's a *nickel*, for goodness sake." She shook her head and started her examination of the old desk. After a moment, she glanced up, pleased to see that Scout and Amber had uncovered a leather chair. "Eww," Amber said. "It's all cracked."

"What did you expect?" Pekin said. "Look how old it is. Think of how it'd look if it hadn't been covered."

She turned back to the desk. There were four small drawers and six vertical slots. The slots were empty, but when she pulled open the top drawer on the left, she found various objects. One by one she removed them from the drawer. A small ball of string, a single silver jack, a marble. After examining each, she returned them to the drawer and moved to the drawer below it. There was a key in the lock, which turned easily, allowing the drawer to slide open. The drawer appeared empty, but when she stuck her hand in, her fingers felt something soft. Pulling it out, she saw it was a black velvet pouch, the fragile fabric powdering under her touch. When she opened the mouth of the bag and turned it upside down, a small amethyst ring fell into her palm. It was too small to belong to a grown woman.

"I think this was Miranda's ring," she said. She held it up, trying to examine it in the dusty light that the grimy windows allowed into the room.

"Can I see?" Amber asked, showing interest for the first time in anything having to do with the house.

Pekin handed it to her friend, who looked at it, then dropped it in Scout's outstretched hand. He studied the inside of the band, then wet his finger and rubbed it around the inside of the band.

"There's some writing," he said. "I can't make it out in here. Let's go outside."

The three of them sat hunched together on the porch. Scout squinted at the ring, then rubbed it, then squinted again. "It says 'M.T. 1915.'"

"Miranda Talbert!" Pekin yelled. "It has to be."

"That makes sense. Especially given its small size. It's so exciting," Amber said, enthusiasm ringing in her voice.

Pekin was happy to see her friend warming up to the adventure. "We should probably put it back. Come on. Let's see what else we can turn up."

She returned the velvet pouch to the drawer where she'd found it. The two remaining drawers were empty. Her mind kept going to the peculiar way the nickel had rolled to the stairs. Like on purpose. Was there something the coin wanted her to see?

"I think I want to check upstairs," she said. She saw Amber's eyes go wide. "You don't have to come with me. Stay down here."

"I don't think you should go alone," Scout said. "If you go, we all go."

Pekin said a heartfelt thanks and started up the stairs, trailed by Scout and Amber, who was grumbling under her breath. Once at the top of the landing, she didn't know what to look for. Everything was the way they'd left it a week before. It was eerily quiet as she moved down the hallway, looking in each room. At Miranda's room, the door, which had slammed shut during their last visit, was open again. Pekin stood in the doorway and peered around, waiting for something to catch her attention.

"We should check the attic again." Before her friends could object, Pekin brushed past them. Climbing the steps to the closed attic door, she turned to see if Scout and Amber were behind her, and opened the door. The attic seemed still and silent. A shiver ran down her back. In a beam of dusty sunlight, something caught her eye, a small red ball sitting in the middle of the floor. She bent and looked closer. The dirty white stars weren't easy to see in the dim light. She straightened. "Hmm."

"What is it?" Scout asked.

She shook her head. "Nothing, I guess. I'm pretty sure I kicked that ball over into a corner last weekend, but I must be wrong." She took one final look around. Her eyes landed on Amber's anxious face. "We can go back downstairs now," she said.

"You don't have to tell me twice," Amber said, with obvious relief.

Pekin backed out of the room and closed the door, then followed her friends downstairs.

The light was starting to fade in the rooms when they reached the ground floor. Pekin wasn't sure what they could accomplish by staying any later. Scout and Amber both looked as tired as she felt. As she bent to pick up her backpack, a chill caused her to straighten and whirl toward the stairway as a bump, bump, bump grew louder. The red ball with white stars came into sight, bouncing down the stairs. Amber screamed and grabbed Scout's arm.

Pekin's breath caught in her throat as the ball stopped at her feet. She glanced at her friends, then bent to pick it up. It felt like the temperature in the room had dropped by twenty degrees in a matter of seconds.

"Pekin, *don't*," Amber hissed as she clutched Scout's arm, pulling him toward the front door. "Let's get out of here!"

The ball was like ice in Pekin's fingers. "I closed that door, right?" she asked as she stared at the ball.

"Yeah, you did," Scout answered. "Amber's right. This is too creepy for me."

Pekin didn't move. *What did it mean?* Now that she was faced with apparent proof of a ghostly presence, something she'd hoped to find, she was freaked out. But also fascinated. The ball grew warm in her hands. Her fight or flight reflex battled with her curiosity. The ball was warming up. *Could it be a sign of friendship?*

"I'll be back," she said to the house as she set the ball down and watched it roll back to the staircase. "I'll be back, Miranda."

She joined her friends huddled on the front walk.

"Aren't you scared?" Amber was doubtful. "You don't look scared. How can you not be scared?"

"I don't know what I am. I'm kind of freaked out, but nothing bad happened. I think Miranda reached out to me, like she was trying to say it was okay for us to be there."

"Where did you come up with that interpretation?" Scout asked. "You speak *ghost* now?"

"Very funny. I didn't feel threatened. Did you? We have to come back tomorrow."

"No way," Amber said, her mouth set in a grim line.

Pekin put her hands on her hips and glared at Amber. "Don't be silly, Amber. You *said* you were in. We were hired to do a job. We can't stop at the first hint of.... whatever it's a hint of."

"I'm not sure I want to go back in there either," Scout said. "We don't have a clue what we're doing. If there *is* a ghost in there, what are we supposed to do with it? We don't know anything about getting a ghost to go to the light, or whatever it is they're supposed to do."

"I've been reading up on it. We need to find out why Miranda's stuck here and fix it. Then she'll be able to move on. Will you at least consider coming back with me?"

"Hey, if you choose to come back here, that's your business," Amber said, stubbornly crossing her arms.

"We've gone through this a million times already. You say you're in, then some little thing happens and you say you're out. If you want out, then *fine*. Let's go home." Pekin straightened her shoulders as she marched toward the car and climbed in the backseat.

The silence as they drove toward home was like a fourth passenger in the car until Scout said, "That was weird, huh?"

Neither Pekin nor Amber answered.

"Was it just me, or did it get cold in there all of a sudden?" he asked.

"It was *really* cold," Amber offered, shivering.

"Do you think it was really a ghost, Ducky?" Scout asked.

"Don't call me that," Pekin growled. "Pekin Duck. Pekin Duck. Nobody's called me that since middle school. And I didn't like it *then*." She huffed and turned toward the car window.

"I'm sorry. I was just trying to lighten you up, Pekie."

"Don't call me *that* either," she said, not quite as stiffly.

"We're sorry, Pekie," Amber tossed in, turning and winking at Pekin.

"We're *in*, okay," Scout said in a gruff voice. "We'll *try* not to let *Miranda* scare us away next time." He glanced at Pekin in the rearview mirror. "Okay?"

"Okay," Pekin said, meeting his dark eyes in the mirror.

"Now that *that*'s settled, wanna grab something to eat on the way home? I think my parents are going to a movie so I'm on my own for dinner."

"Sure," Pekin said. "I'm starved."

"Cool," Scout said.

"I wish I could, but I've gotta get home," Amber said. "My mom wants me home for dinner.

"Are you sure? Come on," Pekin pleaded, with no luck.

Scout dropped Amber at home, and then he and Pekin headed to Benny's.

Pekin glanced sideways at Scout as he drove. She felt her face flush. She was hanging out with Scout. Alone. On a Saturday night. It was almost like a date. Not quite, but she'd take it.

"You HAVE TO ADMIT, IT'S PRETTY WEIRD, the stuff that happened," Scout said, taking a bite of his burger. "We didn't imagine those things...did we?

"Some might say we did. But I'm pretty sure it wasn't all in our minds. That ball bounced right up to me. I know it was in the attic, and I know the attic door was shut."

"We would have noticed if it was left open. I saw you close it."

"And the way the house shook. That scared me." Pekin shivered at the memory.

"And I swear it told us to get out. Why'd we even go back?"

"Because, it's our job. We were supposed to go back. Nothing tried to hurt us or anything."

"Not so far. Though you don't know it won't."

"I'm sure it won't. We can't quit now. Miranda needs us."

"Your overactive imagination *thinks* Miranda needs us."

Pekin's feelings were hurt. She huffed and narrowed her eyes. "It's not my imagination," she retorted.

"Oh, lighten up. You have to admit you're way more into this than Amber and me. It's always been your thing. We were mildly interested, but you...."

She glared at him.

Changing his tone, he asked, "So, what's your plan now?"

"Huh?"

"For tomorrow. What's your plan for what we do next. Now that you want to become best friends with a ghost."

Pekin smiled. "You and Amber are my best friends. Miranda can be my *second* best friend."

"I don't know how you did it, but you've made me way less afraid of the ghost of Elmwood Manor."

"Stick with me, buddy. You'll be fine." Pekin sipped her Cherry Coke. "I'm glad you're going back with me. I'd be really sad if I had to do all of this by myself."

"Yeah, and can you imagine how happy your sister would be if she had to drive you to Elmwood?"

"Oh, God. I don't even want to think about it. I'm lucky you're an older man with his own car."

"That's me. An older man." He puffed his chest out and smiled. "Lucky for you I like younger women."

Chapter Eleven

C LOSING THE DOOR TO ELMWOOD MANOR after they entered, Pekin said, "Ready to get started?" As she picked up the plastic bags containing the cleaning products she'd brought with her, she spotted the red ball still sitting in the parlor. "I'm going to put this back." Without waiting for a response, she scampered up the stairs and was back in less than a minute. "So, Miranda knows we got her message."

Pekin picked up a bottle of Windex. "What do you think about doing the windows today? It will probably take up all our time, but at least it'll be bright in here when we come back."

"Okay with me," Scout said. "Although I doubt the word 'bright' will ever apply in here."

Amber didn't appear quite as excited about the project. She grumbled under her breath as she tucked a roll of paper towels under one arm and picked up another bottle of window cleaner.

"I'm sorry you guys, about all the cleaning stuff. I know it's not the fun part, but it creeps me out being around all this dirt."

"The *dirt* creeps you out?" Amber asked.

Pekin sighed. "We won't do a lot more. Let's make this room and the room with the desk a little cleaner. We'll leave everything else alone."

"Your big secret about seeing ghosts…it's not as hard to believe after what we've all seen here. Do you think you can still see them?" Scout asked.

"I'm not sure, since I haven't seen any for a few years. I hope I'll be able to see Miranda."

"Given what you've told us and what we've seen, it's kind of like you have a superpower."

Pekin laughed. She stood up straight, hands on hips, feet apart and head held high. "Wonder Woman at your service."

That caused Scout to laugh. "You really are." He stood and hugged her, mussing up her hair with one hand.

She pulled away and straightened her ponytail, then said, "We should get to work."

Amber tapped her on the shoulder. "I think we should have brought a ladder."

She was pointing at the windows, the *tall* windows.

Pekin shook her head. "It's impossible to accomplish an entire task around here. Just once, I'd like to be able to go home feeling like I'd done something meaningful."

"I know what you mean," Scout offered. "It's like we're taking baby steps whenever we try to do something."

Amber suggested standing on the bench from the kitchen to reach the highest points, which gave them the height they needed.

"We need our masks again," Pekin said, stepping up on the bench.

"We need whole body coverings," Amber said, laughing.

"Yeah, like paint coveralls," Scout added.

"Guys, my allowance only spreads so far," Pekin said.

Donning masks, which protected them from not only dust but also fumes from the window cleaner, they buckled down, taking turns standing on the bench. The layers of grime smeared around the glass, and the half dozen rolls of paper towels were going fast.

"Let's go get some lunch," Amber suggested hopefully. "I'm starving."

Scout shrugged. "Okay, but we should do drive-thru. We look like hell." He pinched up a shoulder of Pekin's shirt between his thumb and finger and gave it a shake, covering his nose with his other hand against the cloud of dirt that arose around her.

"Thanks a bunch." She scowled, straightening her shirt.

Outside, Pekin looked back at the house. "If there's a hose around here somewhere, we could squirt off the outside of the windows. That would take care of a lot of the dirt keeping the light out. Can we take a quick look before we go? If there isn't one, maybe I can stretch my allowance to pay for a cheap one."

After all those decades, there was no hose lying in the front yard. Scout suggested checking the old shed in the backyard and led the way to the back gate, which, unfortunately, had a rusted padlock on it.

"We'll have to go out through the mudroom," he said, heading back to the front door.

"Should we wait out here for you?" Amber asked.

"Uh, I guess so," Scout said, looking less than excited to tromp through the house and poke around in the shed by himself.

"I'll go with you," Pekin said. "Amber, you can stay here if you want. I'm sure Miranda can't get you if you're in the front yard."

Amber looked doubtful, then said, "Okay. I'll be out here."

Pekin followed Scout through the house. In the mudroom, they found a couple of keys hanging on pegs on the wall. Scout grabbed them and headed out into the backyard. The shed was solid-looking but very weathered. He quickly found the right key for the lock. The door creaked eerily when he turned the knob and pushed it open.

Inside, the dark shed smelled of mold and decay. Scout backed out, digging a flashlight out of his backpack. Flicking it on, he shined the beam around the interior, which contained a myriad deteriorating and stained cardboard boxes, their contents spilling out onto the dirty floor. Cobwebs were everywhere and stretched from a grime-covered window to anything and everything stacked beneath it, giving a spooky cast to the interior of the room as the light panned around. The years and the rats had destroyed most everything in the shed, including the cracked and stiff garden hose which sat coiled inside the door.

"It's bigger in here than I thought it would be."

He flashed the beam on the hose for Pekin's benefit, shrugging as he shut off the flashlight and pulled the shed door closed.

"I guess we need your allowance after all," he said with a crooked grin.

Chapter Twelve

After lunch and a stop at the hardware store, they headed back to Elmwood Manor where Scout screwed the new hose onto the faucet and tested the nozzle.

"It's cool Elonia made sure the electricity and water were on for us. I imagine they've been off for a bunch of years." Pekin sidestepped the spray that came perilously close to where she stood.

"I don't think she had much choice," Scout replied. "We wouldn't get very far if we didn't have lights and water. But, yeah, it's cool."

Amber volunteered to do the outside window washing. Pekin knew Amber would do anything to stay out of the house.

Pekin and Scout headed back inside, leaving Amber wrestling with the hose on the front lawn.

Pekin ran the water in the kitchen sink until it was hot, then added dishwashing liquid to a large bucket, which she lugged back to the front room once it was filled with sudsy water. She set to work washing down the window ledges, trying to remove every last trace of the spider webs that adorned the windows. They made some progress on the windows, and the sunlight that shone in made the interior of the house a little less formidable.

Even standing on the kitchen bench, Pekin couldn't reach the top of the windows, and they looked half-finished. Pekin stood with her hands on her hips contemplating their options, and came up with a foolproof plan. Or so she thought.

"Scout, what do you think about me sitting on your shoulders so I can reach the top of the window?"

"That's a really dumb idea, Pekin. Do you want to break your neck and join Miranda wandering the halls of Elmwood Manor for eternity?"

"You're strong. You can hold me up."

"My answer is no."

She scowled at him, then looked around the room and saw another opportunity. "Okay, then, we could put that footstool on the bench and stand on that. It's sturdy."

Scout climbed off the bench and examined the fabric-cushioned stool. He jiggled it and picked it up to look underneath. Satisfied, he set it on top of the bench.

He turned to Pekin. "Okay, but I'm standing on it, not you."

"But you have bigger feet than I do," she reasoned. "I'll fit better on it."

"I'm taller and I can reach the top of the window. Can you?"

"I think I can. Besides, you can hold onto me so I don't fall. Deal?"

Scout shook his head in exasperation, but gave in. He handed her a bottle of Windex and tucked a roll of paper towels under her arm. Then he took her hand and helped her climb up onto the bench and then the footstool.

Pekin's eyes grew big as she wobbled on the shaky perch.

"You okay up there?" Scout asked, still holding her hand.

"Yeah." She found her balance, and felt Scout's hands on her waist. For a full two seconds, she allowed herself to appreciate the feeling, hoping she wasn't blushing on the outside from his closeness, then took a deep breath and sprayed the window cleaner over the part of the window that was still dirty. She tore off two paper towels and glanced down at Scout to make sure he had her securely before turning to wipe the window clean.

"Brace yourself. I'm going to let go for a minute," he said, as he bent to pick up the bucket of soapy water and set it on the bench, then rinsed out the washcloth and handed it to her. She took the dripping cloth and he held her again as she attacked the cobwebs that had stubbornly adhered to the frame of the window, secretly hoping the residents of those webs weren't waiting somewhere right out of sight to pounce on her.

"Done," she said, dropping the cloth into the bucket. She put her hands on Scout's shoulders as he helped her down. They stood admiring their work when a sudden chill settled around them. Before they could say anything, a shriek came from the front yard. Scout and

Pekin rushed outside to find Amber lying in the grass, her eyes big.

"What happened?" Scout asked, extending a hand to help her to her feet. "Are you hurt?"

Amber pointed at the window and stammered, "There was a face. I saw a face."

"What kind of face?" Pekin wanted to know.

"The scary kind! It was wavery and vague."

"Was it Miranda?" Pekin asked.

"*I* don't know. It was wavery. And invisible." She brushed at the grass on her bottom. "And did I mention it was scary?"

"If it was invisible you wouldn't have been able to see it," Pekin said logically.

"I could see *through* it. Okay?"

"Well, could you tell if it was a girl or not?"

"No. I couldn't. And I hope I never see it again!"

Pekin sighed in exasperation. She supposed she understood Amber being spooked. She watched as Scout reassured Amber that everything was fine.

"Let's get back to work. We can get a couple more windows done before we quit for the day."

"I'm not going in there," Amber said, her hands on her hips. "I want to go home."

"Amber, come *on*. You can't quit now. The ghost didn't try to hurt you, did it? Now, you've seen it so you don't have to worry anymore."

"That's not the way I see it," Amber said. "Maybe it couldn't come outside. You don't know it won't hurt me if I'm in the house."

"Miranda wouldn't hurt you."

"Miranda! You're always talking about Miranda! You don't know the ghost is Miranda, and you don't know what Miranda wants or if she or it or whatever wants to hurt us."

Scout stepped in to calm her down. "Pekin's right, Amber. It hasn't tried to hurt us, and we've been in the house for hours."

"You're not scared?"

"I don't think so. I don't know what I am, but we started this and I think we should keep going. Let's stay two more hours until 5:00 and then pack up and go. Can you stick it out for two more hours?"

Amber glared at Pekin. "If anything else happens, I'm outta here."

"I promise. If anything else happens, we'll leave immediately," Scout said.

"I promise, too," Pekin added, turning and heading back inside.

"Wait 'til you see what we accomplished," Pekin said with satisfaction. "It's only one window so far, but see what a difference it makes in here?"

"It's fine," Amber muttered, obviously not ready to be jollied out of her mood.

Pekin hugged her. "Honest, Amber, I don't think Mir— I mean, *whoever*, wants to hurt us. Do you want to stay inside with us? You can go back outside and squirt off the windows if you want to."

"I'll just watch for a while," she said.

"Okay. Pull up a chair," Scout said with a smile. "You can put it close to the front door if it makes you feel better."

"Scout and I figured out how to reach the high places," Pekin said. She positioned the footstool on the bench under the second window. She stood on the bench and waited for Scout to hand her the Windex and paper towels.

"It worked great," he said, as he helped Pekin to her perch on the stool. He held her waist as she sprayed and wiped at the window from the top down. When she was done, she handed the paper towels and spray bottle to Scout and he handed her the wrung-out washcloth.

Pekin stood on her tiptoes to reach along the top of the window frame and the cobwebs in the corners of the window, then climbed down and hopped to the floor.

"Want to try it?" she asked Amber.

"I don't think so. There might be spiders."

"Okay. If you're sure," Pekin said. "But it's kinda fun."

"I'm sure you think so," Amber said with a wink.

Pekin managed to wipe the horrified expression off her face before Scout saw it.

She made quick work of the final window, then, as Scout helped her off the bench, it occurred to her that maybe she should be outside squirting the windows, in case the ghost showed itself again.

"I'll go finish squirting off the outside of the windows," she said as she opened the front door. "Let me know if anything happens." She gulped when she realized she might have restarted Amber's fear meter, but apparently Amber was comfortable in her chair by the door.

It felt good to aim the jet of water and watch decades of grime slide down the old windows. When she finished all the windows, she put the hose down and stared at each one, hoping to see a face looking back at her. She was disappointed when nothing, absolutely nothing, happened, so she turned the water off and went back inside.

"Wow, you can see a real difference," Amber said, apparently forgetting to be afraid.

"Yeah!" Pekin high-fived Scout with a smile. "We did a good job."

"It's not so scary in here now," Amber said.

"Does that mean you're on for next Saturday?" Pekin asked.

"I'll let you know."

Pekin raised her voice. "Miranda! Don't scare Amber or she won't come back. Okay?"

Scout and Amber laughed. Until a door slammed upstairs.

"Let's pack up and go," Scout said. "Pekin, don't you dare run upstairs to see what it was."

Pekin tsked. "All right. We've done enough for one day."

She picked up her backpack then casually said, "Maybe we should spend the night here one night."

"*What!*" Amber's face went pale.

"Maybe the good stuff happens after it gets dark. We can bring sleeping bags and sack out on the parlor floor. We'd leave all the lights on. What do you think?"

"I think *not*." Amber stamped her foot.

"That's going a little too far, Pekin, don't you think?" Scout wagged a finger at her. "Quit while you've still got a crew."

"I was only kidding, guys."

"Sure, you were," Amber said. "Once you get an idea—"

"Don't worry, Amber. It was a joke. Oh. I forgot to tell you guys, I did some Google searches last night on Miranda. Do you know there were 25 pages of hits? I waded through a bunch of them until my eyes crossed, but didn't learn much. Who knew there would be so many Miranda Talberts?"

"Cool," Scout said.

"Yeah, but it would have been cooler if I'd turned up something interesting about her. I also searched for missing girls in Springdale in the early 1900s. There were several of them right around the time Miranda went missing. I found a list of names, and Miranda's was on the list, but there wasn't much information about her other than the date she went missing and her age. Not much about the other girls, either. The other ones went missing before Miranda. She was the last one to disappear."

"That's interesting," Scout said. "Were they all in Springdale?"

"No. Just Miranda. The others were from surrounding towns."

"Strange," he said with a shrug. "I wonder if there's any connection."

"I'M HUNGRY," SCOUT SAID. "All this manual labor works up an appetite. You guys want to stop somewhere on the way home?"

"I do," Pekin said. "I'm starving."

Amber bowed out again, winking at Pekin. "Sorry, guys, but I better get home. Do you mind dropping me off?"

"Next Saturday?" Pekin asked Amber before she got out of the car.

"Ask me later in the week," Amber tossed over her shoulder. "Call me and let me know what happens."

"What's going to happen?" Scout asked.

"*Nothing*," Pekin and Amber answered at the same time.

"You guys are weird. So, where do you want to go?"

"Pizza?"

"I was hoping you'd say that."

Pekin felt herself flush with nervous energy. She was spending another night hanging out with Scout. Maybe it would become a habit. Tucking her hair behind one ear, her ponytail long since taken down, she looked out the window of Scout's car hoping he wouldn't notice she was turning red.

He was such a gentleman. He ordered a large pepperoni and two Cokes. He even brought napkins to the table. And, most important, he sat next to her in the booth. Not across from her. She hoped he couldn't hear her heart racing.

To get control of her emotions, Pekin said, "So, who do you think slammed the door?"

"I knew you'd bring that up," he said with a grin.

"You know me too well," she said, giving his shoulder a playful shove. She couldn't help the big smile on her face, and he smiled broadly back.

He put his hand over hers. "I do, you know."

She drew in her breath, not daring to move. Was he holding her hand as a friend, or—?

She wouldn't find out, however, because the server appeared at their table and he let go of her hand.

Scout placed two pieces on her plate before taking two for himself. As she took a bite of the crust, Scout said, "Hey, look out," and tucked a strand of her hair behind her ear. "I was afraid you'd eat it. I hope you don't mind."

"Of course I don't." Pekin felt a warm glow at his touch. Tomorrow, she was sure her face was going to hurt from all the smiling.

"Do you like what we're doing?" she asked.

"I didn't think I would, but I like that tingle I get at the thought of seeing a ghost."

"I know, right? I was really disappointed I didn't see a figure in the window like Amber did."

"Give it time. By the way, how much time do we actually have?"

"What do you mean?"

"We're only going over there on weekends. Isn't our client in a hurry to get this taken care of?"

"I think we're okay. She knows we're high school students so weekends are all we have. I told her we could go more often after school's out for the summer. She said not to worry, that after decades, a few more weeks wouldn't matter."

"Good to know."

"Amber seems to be warming up to this, don't you think?" she asked between bites.

"I don't know that 'warming up' is the right way to say it, but she's coming around. Of course, I don't know how many frights it will take to get her to say 'that's all.'"

"I need to meet Miranda. Maybe if I can show Amber that Miranda doesn't want to hurt us, she'll stop worrying."

"You're assuming a lot, there, Ghostbuster."

She didn't want to agree with him, but he had a point. "I want to go over there after school tomorrow. You know, to try and draw Miranda out. Maybe she'll communicate with me."

"I don't think it's smart to go there alone."

"Are you offering to go with me?" she asked.

"I have a team event after school. The coach is having an end of season get together in the gym."

"Maybe we could go later, after your event? I kind of need you to take me."

"What about your sister or your mom?"

"They wouldn't stay there with me. Not that I'm scared or anything."

"No, not that you're scared," he said.

"Okay, maybe I am, a little."

"We'd be there when it's getting dark," he said. "We'd be cutting it close. Or maybe that's your plan?"

"No. I'm not trying to pull a fast one on you."

"I'm not sure how long the party will go, but if—"

"It's okay. I can go by myself." She was disappointed that her fantasy pizza date with Scout had turned sour. "Don't feel bad if you can't make it. I'll have my mom give me an hour or so and then pick me up again."

"Don't be a martyr," he said.

"Why are you ruining this for me?" she asked before she could stop herself.

When Scout looked taken aback, she said, "I'm sorry. I didn't mean that. You've been great."

He sighed. "If your mom drops you off, I'll come over as soon as I can. I can take you home."

"Really? You'd do that?"

"Sure. I don't think you should be there alone."

"You worried about me?" she asked coyly. "You're so protective."

Scout laughed. "Whatever."

He finished off his Coke and said, "Let's get out of here."

When they got to his car, Pekin said, "Thanks, Scout," and impulsively gave him a hug. Surprised, he hugged her back and didn't let go for a long moment before he pulled away and cleared his throat.

"No problem, Pekie."

She watched him drive away from her house and thought about their night. He held her hand, and he hugged her. Little things, to be sure, but maybe they meant something?

Chapter Thirteen

P EKIN TRUDGED UP THE STAIRS to her room, lost in thought and exhausted. She had to admit she was sort of at a loss. Now that she had her first totally legit haunted house, she didn't know what she'd actually do with a ghost. How could she make Miranda appear to her? If she did appear, then what? Before she discovered a real one, it had seemed like, wave your hand and the ghost would be gone. She couldn't admit that to Scout or Amber. They assumed she knew what she was doing, especially after she told them she'd seen ghosts before.

Miranda was a kid, like her. Maybe she was lonely after all those decades alone. Maybe Pekin could bring books, or maybe she could show Miranda her iPhone. Maybe Miranda would be blown away by the changes she's missed out on.

That was it. She'd sit in the parlor, where the windows were clean so there would be light, and start talking. She'd tell Miranda she was there to help her, ask if she needed a friend. Maybe she'd start reading *Harry Potter* to her. It wasn't much of a plan, but it was all she had.

With that decided, she allowed herself to bask in the glow of her amazing time with Scout. Maybe he liked her? He was sweet. Maybe he was just being nice. Or maybe he liked her. Her heart fluttered at the thought that she'd be alone with him at Elmwood Manor.

AT LUNCH THE NEXT DAY, Amber wanted to know all the details about Pekin's dinner with Scout.

"It went really well. He kind of held my hand for just a minute."

"He did?"

"Just for a minute, though. For *no* reason. Then the pizza came, so he let go. But still."

"Anything else? What did you talk about?"

"Miranda. And Elmwood. I'm going over there after school. Scout's going to join me after his team meeting and give me a ride home."

"See? He's spending his free time with you, *not* Vanessa Dooley."

"Yeah, but probably only because I begged him to."

"Anything else *interesting* happen?"

"I hugged him goodbye and he didn't let me go right away. That's something."

"How did that make you feel?"

"Dreamy. I'm being silly, though. I'm like his little sister."

Amber's attention wandered when Josh Parker walked by and smiled. When she turned back to Pekin, she had a wistful expression on her face.

"He was totally checking you out," Pekin said.

"You think so?" Amber looked in the direction Josh had gone.

"I do. I think he likes you. Scout doesn't look at me like that."

"Yet. He doesn't look at you like that *yet*."

"Probably never."

Amber laughed. "You're going to Elmwood by yourself? Aren't you scared?"

"I don't think so. Besides, Scout's coming by. I should be okay."

"What if something happens before he gets there?"

"I hope it does. That's the point, to find ghosts and help them move on. I have to tell you, Amber, I was really jealous that you got to see the face in the window. I was out there washing windows for half an hour and didn't see a single thing."

"You should be glad you didn't. It's pretty unsettling to see through someone."

"But I *want* to, and it's not like I haven't seen them before. Maybe, because I'll be there by myself, Miranda will show herself. I'm going to be prepared to meet her."

"I'm sorry I'll miss it," Amber said.

"Really? I'm so happy to hear you say that. I would hate it if my best friend wasn't part of my new business, even if she hates ghosts."

"Just keep Miranda away from me."

Pekin laughed. "I'll tell her in no uncertain terms not to scare my friends."

Chapter Fourteen

PEKIN COULD BARELY CONCENTRATE the rest of the afternoon. Her classes dragged on and on, even her favorite business class. She had a free period at the end of the day and used it to get her homework done so she could leave the books in her locker.

She spotted Scout in the hallway, his back to her, and started toward him. She wasn't fast enough, however. Vanessa Dooley sidled up to him, cradling her books against her chest and smiling sweetly up at him. Pekin's mouth dropped open, then she closed it, spinning around and heading in the opposite direction before he noticed her.

Her balloon had officially deflated.

PEKIN DROPPED HER BACKPACK on the floor by the front door and scooted up the stairs to the privacy of her room. Flopping on her bed, she texted Amber. *Scout was talking to Vanessa Dooley. Again.*

She waited a few minutes for a reply until her mother knocked on her door and asked if she was ready to go.

"Just a minute," she called. "I'll meet you in the car."

Would it be silly if she tried to fight fire with fire?

She put on her cutest jeans and a green T-shirt that accented her eyes, never forgetting for a minute that Scout would be there later. She grabbed her supplies and headed to her mom's car.

"Do you need a snack or anything?" her mom asked, handing two granola bars to Pekin.

"Not really, but thanks," she answered as she stuffed them in her backpack and settled into the front seat of the car, hoping her mother wouldn't ask if anything was wrong.

Pekin swung her backpack over her shoulder as she climbed out of the car, racing up the path to Elmwood's front door, before remembering to turn back and thank her mom.

Taking out the old key, she unlocked the door and stepped in. Dust motes danced in the late afternoon sunlight that slanted through the newly cleaned parlor windows.

"Showtime," she said.

Pekin wasn't keen on sitting on one of the sofa's threadbare cushions, but she'd try not to move around much. And she could brush any dust off her butt if she needed to.

She couldn't help thinking about Vanessa Dooley...and Scout. How could she compete with Vanessa? Vanessa was beautiful. She had dark sable hair that fell in waves down her back, and big brown eyes. And her lashes were *this* long. In addition to all *that*, Vanessa was on the school's Prom Committee, was Class President, and Valedictorian. So, not just beautiful, but beautiful and smart. And involved.

Then there was Pekin with mousy blonde hair and hazel eyes. *Hazel.* Nobody ever wrote songs about hazel eyes. Blue eyes, sure. Brown eyes, oh yeah. But nondescript, no color hazel? Not to mention she'd never been interested in school politics or activities. She wasn't a joiner. Pekin was smart too, but no one would know it unless they looked at her report cards.

Pekin knew, absolutely knew, that judging someone by their looks was completely politically incorrect. Woman power ~ YES. Body image ~ NO. But she also couldn't pretend that she wasn't secretly jealous of Vanessa Dooley.

She sighed and rested her chin in her hands. Her elation at being here with Scout, alone...well, it was ruined. She sat up and squared her shoulders. She was here for a reason so she should get to it.

"Here goes nothing."

Pekin made herself as comfortable as she could, trying not to disturb the dust. She pulled *Harry Potter* out of her backpack and set it on the floor by the chair.

Taking a deep breath, she said, "Hi, Miranda. I'm Pekin Dewlap. I'm 15. I'm in high school. You're 14, right? I know you've been stuck in this house for a really long time, and I thought you might be lonely. Was it you who threw the red ball down the stairs and slammed doors?

Was it you Amber saw in the window yesterday? I was sad I didn't get to see you, because I really want to meet you.

"Elonia Collins told me about you. She's your second cousin once removed, or something like that. I'm not sure how it works. Anyway, she's your distant relative. She owns this house now. She thinks there's a ghost here. As soon as she told us about what happened to you all those years ago, I was sure you must be the ghost. My friends and I were sent here to help you leave. If you want to. This is such a lovely house. It needs a family to live here who can appreciate what a beautiful home it could be. But something has scared people away. Maybe it's you?"

Pekin hoped her voice didn't quiver as she talked. In spite of what she'd told her friends, she was nervous about being at Elmwood alone. If a door slammed upstairs, she might just jump up and run out the door. She looked around and sighed, tapping her chin thoughtfully.

"So, anyway. Is there anything you'd like to know about me? I didn't know if you'd talk to me, so I brought a really awesome book to read to you. I thought you might be bored. I don't know what ghosts can or can't do, but I wasn't sure you could read a book by yourself. I'm going to read to you for a little bit. If you feel like you want to make yourself known to me, go for it. I'm hoping we can be friends."

Nothing. She looked around again, then reached down and picked up the book.

"Ahem," she started.

Pekin still loved the story of Harry Potter and his wizard friends, and lost herself in the story for a couple of chapters. After a while, she stopped reading and glanced around. Nothing. Disappointed, she put the book down and walked to one of the newly clean windows. She stood looking out, feeling sorry for herself. At first she saw nothing interesting, but then her eyes fell on a small, round woman standing across the street staring at Elmwood Manor. When the woman saw Pekin looking at her, she clambered into her car and, without looking back, drove away.

Curious, Pekin thought. That woman had looked a lot like Tangina Barrons, the odd little medium in the old 1982 movie *Poltergeist* that she'd watched more than once with her friends. Did the woman also have a tiny, high-pitched little voice like Tangina's? Why was she so interested in Elmwood?

It was probably nothing but her imagination that made Pekin think the woman was staring at Elmwood. She shrugged and went back to the chair.

"Miranda, are you listening? I'm going to read some more of *Harry Potter*. It's about a boy wizard who goes to a magical school. He has two friends, like I do, but his are Hermione Granger and Ron Weasley. My friends are Amber and Scout. I loved *Harry Potter* when I was younger, and I read every one of the books. There are seven of them. Wouldn't it be funny if you liked them, too, and I ended up reading all seven to you? Anyway, you'll love the story. Let me know if you're here, okay?"

She wiggled in her seat to get comfortable, then picked up the book and read further. After a short while, she paused and glanced toward the hallway. "Miranda?"

She was starting to doubt whether her strategy was going to work, but decided to give it a little more time. After all, Miranda had been a ghost for *decades*.

It felt odd to read out loud to an empty room, but Pekin held onto the hope that the room wasn't entirely empty. She continued reading for another five minutes before stopping to explain some of the details of the book.

"Albus Dumbledore is the head wizard at Hogwarts, the magical school. It's such a good story, Miranda. I hope you're listening." She leaned back, dejected and ready to give up.

The temperature in the room dropped dramatically. Pekin jumped up and gasped. "Miranda?"

A shimmer by the parlor door caught her attention. Pekin stared at it, afraid to move.

"Miranda, I saw my grandmother after she passed away. She came and spoke to me, and I could see her. Can you let me see you?"

The shimmer glowed slightly, and Pekin heard bump bump bump as the red ball with white stars bounced down the stairs and rolled up to her feet. She picked it up and smiled.

"Miranda, I—"

"Pekin, it's me," Scout called out as he opened the door.

In an instant, the shimmer disappeared.

Pekin ran to him and threw her arms around his neck. "She was here! I saw her."

"Miranda? You saw Miranda?"

"Well, I *kind of* saw her. I didn't actually *see* her, but the room got super cold, you know the way it gets, and there was a shimmer, there, by the door, and when I asked if it was her, this ball bounced down the stairs and stopped right at my feet." She held up the ball for him to see.

Scout looked skeptical. Pekin sighed and shook her head in exasperation. "It *had* to be her. I'd just told her that I used to see my grandmother after she died and asked Miranda if I could see *her*. Then it got cold and I saw the shimmer. And, no. It wasn't the sun shining in the window on something."

As she stood glaring at him defiantly, hands on her hips, he said, "You're cute when you're stubborn, you know that?"

Completely disarmed by his words, Pekin sniffed, "Oh, I am not," hoping he couldn't hear her heart wildly beating.

"Are, too," he said with a laugh. "What now? Should we hang out and see if she comes back?"

"We could try. I've been reading *Harry Potter* to her."

"No way."

"Yep. I think she must like it. Just when I was ready to quit, she appeared. Or sort of appeared. You know."

"That's a really long book. Are you planning to read the whole thing to her?"

"I don't know. Depends. Anyway, if you sit there quietly while I read she might come back."

He took a seat on the sofa next to Pekin. She picked up the book. "Miranda, I'm going to read some more. Come listen."

She began reading, now and then glancing around the room or looking at Scout. After fifteen minutes, she closed the book.

"Miranda, don't be afraid because Scout's here. He's my friend. He wants to meet you, too."

When nothing happened, Scout said, "We should think about trying again another time. It's going to be dark soon, and I'm pretty sure neither one of us wants to be here after dark."

"Maybe we need to be here after dark."

"You're serious, aren't you?"

"I might be a *little* scared. Unless you stayed, too?"

"Oh, yeah. That would look great. You and me spending the night together in an empty house."

Pekin turned bright red, and she knew Scout noticed this time.

"I didn't embarrass you, did I?"

"Of course not," she said. "Why would I be embarrassed?"

He just looked at her.

"So, you and Vanessa Dooley." Great way to change the subject.

"What?"

"You like her, don't you?"

"Where did *that* come from?"

"You always seem to be talking to her."

"I do not."

"I must be wrong then." She could feel embarrassment creeping over her.

Scout looked at her, his face reflecting confusion.

"First of all, I talk to a lot of people. Vanessa's just one of them."

"She's flirting with you." Pekin knew she should keep her mouth shut, but somehow the words kept tumbling out. "All the time."

"What the hell are you talking about?" Scout's voice rose.

"I've seen you with her more than once."

"Are you jealous?"

"*No.*" Pekin was horrified. Even if she *was* jealous she wouldn't tell him.

"You're being weird," Scout said. "We should go." He stood and walked to the front door.

Pekin watched him, wondering how things had gone so wrong. She picked up her backpack, unzipping it and putting the book inside.

She looked around again. "Miranda, I'm going now. I'll come back and read some more tomorrow, okay?"

She put her hand on Scout's arm. "I'm sorry about...about whatever that was. Being in a haunted house alone can make you act strange."

His eyes were hard. Had she hurt his feelings?

"Are you mad at me?"

"Are you mad at me?" he countered.

"No. But I don't want you to be mad at me because I stuck my nose in your business." She threw her arms around his neck. "Because that's what friends do. Okay?"

He laughed and lifted her slightly with a one-arm hug. "Okay."

He opened the door and stepped out onto the porch. "Don't be disappointed, Pekie. You made some progress."

"I'm not. I can't expect to see immediate results. I want her to trust me enough to come out next time I'm here." She set the red ball down at the foot of the stairs. "Thanks for the ball, Miranda. I'll leave it here for you. See you soon."

Chapter Fifteen

"It was so rad, Amber. I'm pretty sure I saw Miranda." Pekin lay on her bed, her cell on speaker mode.

"What did she look like?"

"It was a shimmery thing, but I'm sure it was Miranda. I was reading *Harry Potter* to her and—"

"Wait. You were reading *Harry Potter* to a ghost?" Her voice sounded skeptical.

"Yes. It's perfect. She's a kid like us, and she's been locked in that old house all by herself for, like, ever. She must be bored out of her mind. Don't you think?"

"I suppose. But—"

"I want to make friends with her. I can read to her. I'm going to play some cool music for her, so she can see what kids are into today. And I can show her videos on my iPad. Wouldn't you like to see stuff like that if you'd been alone in a haunted house since the early 1900s?"

"She's the one haunting it," Amber, always the practical one, pointed out.

"Still, she's got to be lonely. This will work. I know it."

"Won't you get tired of reading to her? I mean, *seven* volumes."

"Let's not get ahead of ourselves. We'll see how it goes. Besides, I can stop after the first one."

"Hmm."

"Would you want to go over there with me tomorrow after school?"

"Um—"

"Or some other day this week?"

"I don't know. Maybe. We can talk about it tomorrow."

Pekin took a deep breath. "I had a fight with Scout."

"You did? Why?"

"I saw Vanessa Dooley talking to him today. You should have seen the way she was gazing into his eyes. She probably batted her eyes at him, too."

"And?"

"And I may have brought it up."

"Carefully?"

"Probably not. I blurted out that he was talking to her all the time."

"Did he try to explain?"

"No. He said I was jealous."

"Well, you *are* jealous."

"I'm going to have to accept that he has a girlfriend now."

"Oh...my...god. You're already marrying him off to Vanessa Dooley, aren't you?"

"Don't be silly. But, still, every time I turn around, there he is talking to Vanessa Dooley."

"How many times have you seen him talking to her?"

"Um, two?"

"Wow. I can see the problem. He *must* be in love with her since he talked to her twice."

"You're not very sympathetic."

Amber laughed. "I'm your best friend. Of course, I'm sympathetic. If you have to obsess about something, obsess about seeing Miranda. You're blowing the Vanessa thing way out of proportion."

Pekin didn't say anything for a moment. "You're right. I suppose I might be premature about Scout and his new girlfriend."

"You're hopeless. I'll see you at school tomorrow."

Pekin put down her phone and curled into a ball around Griselda. "You're sympathetic, aren't you?" she asked the little gray cat snuggled in her arms.

Chapter Sixteen

EKIN WAS NERVOUS ABOUT SEEING SCOUT. She wondered if he'd join her and Amber at lunch like he normally did. Amber was waiting for Pekin in the cafeteria, and they went through the line together. Scout appeared as they were heading for a table and waved from the end of the lunch line.

"Do you think he's mad at me?" Pekin asked, watching Scout as he made his way along the line.

"He waved, didn't he? I think he's fine. If you don't act weird, he won't."

"Tell me if I start acting weird or babble or anything, okay?"

"Okay, but you'll probably know it if it happens. Don't *worry*. Just be normal."

When he joined them, Scout seemed fine. He gave his usual Scout smile, and Pekin dared to be hopeful that he'd forgotten, or at least forgiven, what she said to him the night before. But there was still that tickle of anxiety she couldn't quite banish.

Amber chattered away, probably to fill in the gaps. Pekin wasn't normally quiet, but she was embarrassed over her outburst with Scout and couldn't manage much small talk. She smiled a lot and hoped he didn't notice she was anxious.

SINCE NEITHER SCOUT NOR AMBER was available to go with her after school, Pekin had to go back to Elmwood by herself. She turned down her mother's offer to keep her company, worried that Miranda wouldn't appear if anyone was in the house with her.

Pekin did a sweep of the ground floor, calling out "Miranda" in each room she entered. Receiving no response, she headed back to the parlor and dug *Harry Potter* out of her backpack.

"Hi, Miranda. I'm back." She picked up the ball she'd left lying on the floor in the parlor the night before. "It was great to see you yesterday. I told Scout and Amber all about it. I think they were jealous they didn't get to see you.

"I got mad at Scout after he picked me up yesterday. There's this girl at school, Vanessa Dooley, and I can tell she likes him. What if he likes her back? Did I tell you that *I* like Scout? He just thinks of me as a friend though. A best friend, but still...."

She sat on the sofa, careful not to raise any dust. "You probably don't want to hear about that, since you don't know Scout, other than seeing him here with me. If you do decide to reveal yourself to Scout, please don't tell him what I said, okay?"

Pekin sighed and opened the book. "I'm going to continue reading. Please come join me. I know you'll love this book." She looked several times toward the doorway, but no shimmer appeared. Refusing to be disappointed, she settled into the cushions and opened the book to the place she'd left off the day before. After two chapters, she closed the book. Maybe a little conversation would be more appealing to the ghost girl.

"I had lunch with Scout and Amber today. I hope maybe we can all be friends. I know you'd like them. Amber is sooo nice. We've been friends since the second grade. She's kind of scared of you. I keep telling her you won't hurt us. You won't, right? Anyway, she's one of the partners in my company. I have my own business, and the owner of your house, your cousin Elonia, is my first client. We try to help spirits move on. I don't want to kick you out of your house, but it isn't right for you to be stuck here when you should be with your friends and family on the other side. Anyway, then there's Scout. We won't talk about him, since I already told you about Vanessa Dooley. Amber, Scout and I grew up together. I was afraid Scout might still be mad, but he was fine at lunch. He probably just thinks I'm weird. I'm not sure if he likes me back. In that way, I mean. Don't you think he's cute? I'm so excited that he likes coming here with me. At least I think he does."

She opened the book again and read another chapter. Then stood and left the book on the sofa. Dejected, she walked to the window. She did a double-take when she saw the little round woman again sitting in her car staring at Elmwood Manor. "Who *is* that woman?"

With a start, Pekin felt a wave of frigid air at the same time she saw the reflection of a small blonde girl in the window. Her first instinct was to turn around, but she didn't want to scare Miranda away. Instead, she said quietly, "What do you think she wants?"

In the reflection, she saw the girl look up at her. Even more quietly, Pekin said, "I can see you. You won't vanish if I turn around, will you?"

The little blonde girl didn't respond, so Pekin slowly turned. The translucent image of a little girl shimmered in front of her.

Pekin wouldn't give in to the urge to be afraid. "Hello, Miranda. I'm Pekin. I'm so glad to get to see you."

When the form didn't dissolve, she said, "Should I keep reading?"

The blurry form seemed to glide to the sofa where Pekin had been sitting and hovered as if waiting. Pekin sat and picked up the book. She read several pages, then stopped and said, "I'm so happy you're here. We can have so much fun together."

Pekin read on, now and then glancing at the transparent girl, who seated herself beside Pekin on the sofa. The ghost appeared to relax.

After a time, she closed the book and looked at her phone. Pekin looked shyly at Miranda. "It's almost time for me to leave. Will I see you if I come back?" She got no answer, but continued. "I want you to meet my friends. Can you let them see you, too? If you give them a chance, you'll like them. Don't be scared of them. Or of me. Okay?"

As she stared at the translucent girl, she heard a honk and the ghost disappeared. She glanced once more around the room, and picked up her backpack. "Goodbye, Miranda," she said as she closed the door.

Chapter Seventeen

After dinner, Pekin settled down at her desk and grabbed her phone, which started to vibrate as soon as she touched it.

"How'd it go today?"

She was surprised to hear Scout's voice. It was usually Amber who called. She was almost too overcome with emotion to speak rationally. The words crowded each other out and Scout told her to slow down so he could understand her.

"Sorry," she said. "It's just, I saw her today!"

"Miranda?"

"Yes. It was amazing. I was reading to her and took a break and wandered over to look out the window, and I saw her reflection in the window behind me. She was still there when I turned around. She's *adorable*."

"A ghost is adorable." He sounded like he was rolling his eyes.

"You know what I mean. She's kind of tiny. She had on this cute dress and bows and she has blonde hair in curls. And Mary Janes. You know what those are, right?"

"Some kind of shoes?"

"Yes. Dressy ones."

"Then what?"

"Then I started reading to her again, and she came and sat beside me. She didn't disappear until my mom honked."

"Wow. That's really cool. I wish I could see her, too."

"I told her I wanted her to meet you and Amber, and asked if you could see her, too. Can you go after school tomorrow?"

"Yeah, maybe."

"Great. I'll meet you at your car after school. Hopefully I can get Amber to go with us."

"It's a plan."

"Oh, Scout. I have chills when I think about it. I can't believe it happened."

"I almost can't either," he said. "Okay. Talk to you tomorrow."

Pekin immediately called Amber. She knew Amber was afraid, but she detected a note of excitement in her best friend's voice as she told her about seeing a ghost. *Their* ghost. And, best of all, Amber agreed to go to Elmwood Manor with them.

CHAPTER EIGHTEEN

T HE THREE STOOD NERVOUSLY on the porch as Pekin pulled out the old key.

"You fixed the number," Amber said, running her finger over the 2.

"Scout did. It looks so much better now." Taking a deep breath, Pekin unlocked the door. "Ready?" she asked over her shoulder. Sticking her head inside, she called out, "Miranda?"

No response. She stepped into the entryway, followed by Scout and Amber.

"Do you think she'll come out?" Amber asked. She stood behind Scout, peeking around him as if reluctant to be too exposed.

"I hope so. Yesterday, she came after I started reading. Get comfortable, and I'll see if it works today."

Pekin removed her book from her backpack and sat in one of the parlor chairs.

"Miranda, it's me again, Pekin. I brought my friends Scout and Amber with me, like I told you. They want to meet you and hope you'll come out again."

She looked around hopefully, but saw nothing out of the ordinary. "We want to be your friends. We thought since you've been alone for such a long time you'd be happy to have company. And if you're stuck here and can't move on, we can help you do that. If you want, we can play some music for you. It's really different from what you listened to when you were, you know, still around. Today's music is awesome. I'm sure you'll like Taylor Swift. She has super cool stuff. And hip hop. It will blow your mind."

She pulled her iPhone out of her back pocket and scrolled through her playlist. "What do you guys think? Should we start with easy stuff like Bruno Mars or Taylor or something? Or do some Maroon 5 or The Weekend?"

"We don't want to scare her," Amber said. "It's been quiet in here for a billion years. You shouldn't start blaring something too raw."

"Yeah, I think Amber's right on that. Play something by Taylor Swift. It's good singalong and dance music."

Soon the parlor was alive with "Shake It Off." Pekin twirled around, moving in time to the beat of the music. "Come on, you guys. Let's dance. Maybe she'll see how much fun it is and join us."

Amber was doubtful and Scout didn't jump to his feet, so Pekin launched into her favorite dance moves. "I feel pretty silly up here by myself," she said, glaring at her friends. She grabbed Amber's hand and pulled her to her feet. With a little prodding, Amber was dancing with Pekin, and they both looked at Scout, who reluctantly slouched onto the floor. In moments, all three were singing along and mindlessly moving around to the music. By the time "Bad Blood" started playing, they were having too much fun to notice the chill when the air in the room turned cold.

Until Amber's eyes grew big. Pekin followed her gaze to the doorway. It was very faint, just a shimmer in the air, but a vague shape was forming. Amber said "Oh!" and her hand flew to her mouth, as Pekin tried to shush her. Scout, dancing, was oblivious to what was going on until Pekin pulled on the sleeve of his T-shirt.

"What?" he asked, still into the song.

"Look," she said, motioning with her head.

When he did, his mouth fell open and he stopped mid-step.

"Keep dancing. Don't scare her away." One by one, they started dancing again, and they watched as, unbelievably, the shimmery girl began to move with them.

When the song ended, the kids smiled in the direction of the translucent form they were sure was Miranda. And then collapsed in giggles onto the floor. The ghost floated to the floor as well.

"It would be cold in here if we weren't so hot from dancing," Amber said.

"Yeah. It's like having air conditioning," Pekin added.

Everyone seemed to be waiting to see what would happen next.

Scout stepped up. "I'm Scout," he said. "Very pleased to meet you."

Amber, who'd momentarily forgotten to be afraid, said, "Me, too. I'm Amber."

The shape flickered and grew fainter, a translucent stain in the air.

Pekin approached it and held out her hand. "Miranda, are you okay?"

"Don't go," Amber said. "We just met you."

There was a disturbance in the air, and the form grew more solid. They could see through her, but they could also see blonde curls tied back with a blue ribbon. A taffeta party dress of pinks and blues, white stockings and black patent leather Mary Janes. And a teenager's pretty face. A face that was smiling.

Pekin stepped back in awe. When she looked at Amber and Scout, their faces reflected the amazement she felt.

Even more amazing, the ghost reached out her hand and touched Pekin's face. *Friends*, she said.

Pekin touched her hand to her cheek. She could swear she felt something. Not a touch, exactly, but a *sensation* of some kind.

"Yes, Miranda. Friends."

And then Miranda was gone.

"Where did she go?" Scout asked, glancing around the room.

"Wow! Just *Wow!*" Amber said. "Can you believe it?" She was hopping up and down as she followed Scout and Pekin into the hallway to retrieve their backpacks.

"I *know*," Pekin said.

Amber still hadn't come down from her excitement by the time Scout dropped her at home. "When can we go back?" she asked.

Even Scout was eager to see what would happen next.

"Should we try for tomorrow after school?" Pekin asked.

"My mom wants me to help her with some stuff tomorrow," Scout said.

"Then maybe Saturday? We should all be together when we go see Miranda. Does that work?"

"It works for me," Amber said.

"Me, too," Scout offered.

"I'm freaked out about today," Pekin asked. "It's so worth it, isn't it?"

"To see something as amazing as that?" Scout's face reflected the awe Pekin knew all of them felt. "Oh, yeah."

"I didn't really believe there'd be a ghost," Amber said. "I didn't believe in ghosts at all. And I thought they'd be creepy. You know, if there were any. But Miranda's not creepy. She's so *cute.*"

Chapter Nineteen

"What if she doesn't show up?" Amber asked as they dropped their backpacks by the front door of Elmwood.

"She will." Pekin tried to project certainty, hoping her friends would buy it.

"Shouldn't we have a plan? We can't keep on having dance parties with Miranda, can we?" Scout, the voice of reason.

"I've thought about it since our last visit. My mom wanted to know the same thing. She was worried Elonia would run out of patience since it's taking so long."

"But we have *school*," Amber whined.

"I know. Elonia knows that. I assured her that we'd work hard once school was out."

"Do you have a plan, though?" Scout asked again.

"What if...I don't know, maybe we spend a couple more days winning Miranda's confidence. I can read to her some more, we can do the dance thing. Scout, you could take out your laptop. You have a bunch of videos on there. Maybe we could get her to watch a movie with us? Anyway, as soon as school's out, we'll try to have a real conversation with her. Ask her what's keeping her here. How we can help her leave, if she wants to. That kind of thing. Anyway, that's what I was thinking."

"It's not a bad plan. In fact, I think it's a good plan. We definitely don't want to come on too strong right away and scare her away. Amber, what do you think?"

"It's okay, I guess. Let's do that."

It had seemed cold when they entered Elmwood. Cold and empty. "Maybe we're expecting too much," Pekin said. "We'll talk for a while and see what happens."

In the parlor, Pekin sat in one chair and Scout pulled up the other one while Amber sat on the sofa.

"Miranda, we're back. Can you come out?" Pekin said.

"Hi, Miranda," Amber added. "Can't wait to see you. It will be so fun."

"It's very weird, Amber," Pekin said. "You were afraid to come with us before, and now you're excited to be here."

"I've never met a ghost before. Of course I was scared."

"I'm not complaining. In fact, I'm super happy about it. I was worried you wouldn't want to be a Ghostie with me."

"A 'Ghostie?'" Scout asked.

"Don't you remember our ghost club?"

"Sure. We were *eight*."

"So? It still works."

"Do we have to wear sheets again?"

Pekin ignored his comment. "I thought that would be a good name for us. You know, since we're in the business of finding ghosts and all. 'Ghostbusters' is already taken. Do you have a better name for us?"

"I don't know, but something not so frilly."

"Ghostie is frilly?"

"We could be 'Ridders,'" Amber offered. "Because we rid the haunted houses of their ghosts."

"Do you think we should be talking about getting rid of ghosts in front of a ghost?" Scout said, practical as always.

"Oh, I forgot," Pekin said. "She isn't here yet, so far as we know. Maybe she didn't hear it."

She pulled out *Harry Potter* and read a few pages, then looked around. No sign of Miranda.

"Let's try the music," Amber said.

Pekin pulled her phone out of her pocket and scrolled through her titles. "Same kind of music as last time?" she asked. Scout and Amber nodded in agreement. Ariana Grande's "Bang Bang" filled the room with a catchy beat.

"Good one," Scout said, flashing a thumbs-up.

Pekin started singing along first, and was soon joined by Amber. As the song ended and another began, Pekin said, "Scout, get up and dance. We have to make this look fun."

He was the first to notice when a chill fell over the room. "I think she's here," he said under his breath.

Pekin and Amber looked around. "There she is," Amber said, her voice squeaky with excitement.

Just a shimmer at first, but they all saw it.

"Hi, Miranda," Pekin said.

"Come play with us," Amber said. "We're having so much fun."

"Do you want me to read to you, or do you like dancing? Or do you want to see a video?"

"I'm pretty sure she doesn't know what a video is, Pekin," Scout said.

"Oh, right. But she probably knows what a movie is."

"Can you pull up some cute animal videos on YouTube, Scout?" Amber asked.

The shimmer didn't come any closer and the lights flickered.

"Whoa. I think we're overwhelming her," Pekin said. "Let's all sit down and I'll read to her."

They made themselves comfortable again and Pekin delved into the story, now and then glancing up to see if it was having any effect. In a short time, Miranda moved into the room and hovered at Pekin's chair, slowly becoming visible as the young girl she was.

After a while, Pekin stretched and closed the book. "What should we do now?"

"Can we watch animal videos?" Amber asked.

"You'll like this, Miranda," Pekin addressed the ghost. "Watch what Scout's doing." Scout flipped open his laptop and found a baby animal video and hit Play. Pekin and Amber sat beside him on the sofa and Pekin gestured to Miranda to join them. As she approached and looked at the screen of the laptop, Miranda audibly gasped and put her hand over her mouth. She backed up and started to fade, the lights in the room going crazy.

"Don't go," Pekin said. "Miranda, it's like watching a movie, a film. A modern one. It's baby animals. Aren't they cute? You'll love them." She pleaded with the form that had become a vague outline.

The outline drifted closer to the kids, tentatively looking at Scout's laptop. As she focused on the video playing on the screen, Miranda became visible again, and laughed, an odd, echo-y sound. She reached out as if to touch the picture, but her hand passed through the screen.

Pekin heard a car door outside and looked out the window. "My mom's here," she said.

She turned to Miranda. "My mom would like to meet you. Will you stay and say 'hi' to her?"

Miranda grew fainter.

"Please, Miranda? I want my mom to know it's safe for me to be here. I want her to see that you're okay with us. Can you stay?"

Yes, Miranda answered softly.

Pekin's mom, Melissa, followed Scout into the parlor, then gasped and took a step backward as she became aware that she could see through one of the kids.

Pekin jumped up. "It's okay, Mom. This is Miranda. I told her I wanted you to meet her. It's really okay." Pekin was concerned her mother would freak out, but Melissa took a deep breath and replied, "I'm fine."

She looked shaken as Pekin led her into the room, but managed a tentative smile. "It's nice to meet you, Miranda." She started to extend her hand, but realized when Miranda glanced at it nervously that it wasn't a good idea.

Still slightly dazed, Melissa took a seat on the sofa, not able to take her eyes off the ghost.

"Is it okay if I talk to Miranda?" she asked.

"Of course, Mom."

Melissa cleared her throat. "Miranda, dear, thank you for letting me see you. I hear bits and pieces from Pekin, but to see you myself…it's very special." She smiled shakily, and Miranda smiled back in her wavery way. "When I was young, I could see ghosts, too, but I guess I outgrew it. It's a pleasure to have this experience again."

Not knowing what else to say, Melissa stood. "I should be going. She turned to Pekin and gave her a hug. "I'll see you at dinner."

She started to turn toward the door, but stopped. "Miranda, I'm happy to get a chance to meet you."

And I as well, Miranda responded.

CHAPTER TWENTY

PROM WAS THE FOLLOWING WEEK. It was a combined prom, junior and senior wrapped up into one party. Amber was positively glowing about being asked by Josh Parker. Pekin understood how she felt. The way *she* would feel if she were going with Scout. She felt a pang that she wasn't going to the dance with Scout. He hadn't asked her, though. Allen Torkelson had.

Pekin didn't have a crush on Allen. He'd been a schoolmate all through high school. He was funny and sweet, and Pekin felt that perhaps Allen liked her, but up until now she hadn't been sure.

Would Scout have gone with her if she'd asked him? She kicked herself for missing the opportunity. What if he'd said no and then everything was weird between them. She supposed it was best that she was going with Allen.

She decided not to let her disappointment bring her down. The dance would be fun, and shopping with an extremely excited Amber would be a blast.

Pekin was determined to find a dress that would make her look older and glamorous. If Scout showed up at the dance with Vanessa Dooley, Pekin wanted to make sure he noticed her. She wanted to make him jealous.

Amber gushed about Josh the entire time they were at the mall. Did Pekin think Josh would like this dress? Would he like that dress? "I have to look *fabulous*," she said. "This is my future we're talking about."

"I'm not sure it's your *future*, but that one's adorable," Pekin said, trying to sound enthusiastic about the baby blue spaghetti-strap dress Amber was modeling. Rhinestones adorned the bodice and the light in the dressing room reflected off them. The dress looked great on her, and Pekin knew Amber was picturing Josh's face when he saw her in it.

"Now can you help *me* look fabulous?" she asked Amber. "You know, in case…Scout's there."

Amber stopped swirling in front of the mirror. "You should have asked him."

"I was too embarrassed. Besides, what if he said no? Every time I see him, I'll feel like curling into a ball and disappearing. I don't want to ruin our friendship. What if I lose him?"

"That won't happen. Scout *loves* you."

"Yeah, sure. Like he'd love a puppy. Do you think he's going with Vanessa Dooley?"

"No. But, just in case, let's find a fabulous dress for you, too."

Pekin swiped through the racks of fancy dresses, pulling one and then another out to scrutinize, then putting them back on the rack, nothing quite what she was looking for. Until, hanging at the end of an aisle, as if on display, Pekin saw a long, black satin gown with a sweetheart neckline. Pekin and Amber pointed to it at the same time and said "That's it."

Pekin tried it on, twirling around, excited. "It's *perfect*. It makes me feel beautiful," she said, at last feeling excited for the dance.

BUSY WITH END-OF-SCHOOL-YEAR ACTIVITIES, they hadn't been back to Elmwood for most of a week. Three days before prom was the first time they could visit.

Miranda's shimmery form greeted them at the front door as they arrived.

She smiled when the music started. Scout held out his hand to Miranda. "Would you like to dance with me?"

Even though she couldn't take his hand, her pale, translucent face lit up in a smile. She tried to copy the moves Pekin and Amber were making as she turned delightedly around the floor, always near Scout. When the song ended, Pekin offered to teach Miranda how modern kids danced.

It was funny to see a girl and a ghost trying out dance moves. Miranda watched intently, and, despite her early awkwardness, she did her best to emulate the way Pekin and Amber moved to the music.

"This is good practice," Amber said to Miranda. "Our prom is Thursday. I'm going with Josh. He's so cute. I can't wait." She spun around giggling. "You should see my dress!"

"Do you know what a prom is?" Pekin asked.

Like a party?

"Yes. Exactly like a party. At school," Amber said.

Miranda said, *I'm sure it will be wonderful.*

"Pekin's going, too," Amber said. "She's going with Allen. He's going to be really surprised when he sees her in her dress. If he didn't like her before—"

Aren't you going with Scout? Miranda asked Pekin.

Scout looked at her. "Uh, no. Another boy asked me." She cleared her throat, praying her red cheeks weren't obvious. "Are you going, Scout?"

"I haven't decided," he said. He frowned and turned away.

Pekin wasn't sure whether she wanted him to go or not. Although she'd be disappointed if he wasn't at the dance, it would be *awful* to see him with Vanessa Dooley, so she didn't press him.

"You *have* to go," Amber said. "Wait 'til you see Pekin. She's going to be—"

"*Amber.*" Pekin looked horrified.

"What? You're going to look really beautiful. Scout should see you."

Amber looked between Scout and Pekin. "Oh, come on, you guys. Lighten up."

Miranda watched silently, concern in her eyes.

"We should take pictures to show Miranda later," Amber said. "Speaking of pictures, can we take your picture, Miranda?"

Miranda was silent, shimmering. She nodded.

"Cool," Amber said.

Pekin pulled her phone out of her back pocket, thankful for the change of topic. "You guys stand by the window. "No," she said, tapping her chin as she watched the three of them gather in the light streaming through the window. "It's too washed out. Try by the front door."

She positioned Amber and Scout and pointed to where Miranda

should join them. Looking through the viewfinder, all three were in the picture, but she wasn't altogether sure that once the button was clicked there would still be three. She snapped several shots from different positions, then pulled up the photos on her phone. "Yeah!" she said, followed by a fist-pump.

Amber and Scout rushed to look over her shoulder at the photos. Pekin turned her phone around to show Miranda, who looked for a long moment at the pictures, as if spellbound.

Thank you, she said softly.

"No. Thank *you*," Pekin responded. "It is so great to have a picture of you."

"Can you send them to us?" Amber asked.

"You can't show anybody if I do," Pekin said.

"Why not?" Amber whined. "I want to show Josh."

"You especially can't show Josh. You can't tell Josh anything."

"That's not fair."

"God, can you imagine if people found out about this? We can't have a bunch of people rushing over here to see Miranda. We can't tell anyone about this. At least not until we're done."

"I have to agree with Pekie," Scout said. "First of all, do you want all our friends to think we're crazy? And if they don't, that might be worse. You know they'd show up here and try to get in to see the haunted house."

The ghost looked horrified and the lights flickered.

"Look. You scared her," Pekin said to Amber.

"I did not. Scout scared her."

"Me? What did I do?" Scout asked with a frown.

"At least wait a while to see how your relationship with Josh goes," Pekin said.

Amber scowled.

"Really, Amber. You have to promise. Look how long it took before Miranda trusted us. How do you think she'd feel if people started tromping in and out of here? It's not fair to expose her to that."

Amber still scowled, but finally said, "Okay, *fine*. I promise."

"Don't pout either," Pekin said with a grin.

"It's getting late. We should pack up." She picked up her backpack, then set it down again. "Miranda, we may not be back for a while. We have the prom and lots of end-of-year activities. We're going to be busy. But, in another week school will be out and we'll have all day to spend with you. There are things we need to talk to you about."

"But we'll bring pictures of the prom to show you," Amber added as she slung her bag over her shoulder.

"See you later," Scout added, and headed out the door.

Pekin locked the door after her friends were out, and joined them in the car. Amber let her have the front seat.

"Are you sure I can't tell Josh—"

"Amber, I swear...you know why we can't talk about this to anyone. Is that the only thing you can think of to talk about with Josh?"

"No, I suppose not."

Pekin shook her head in exasperation. She looked over at Scout. He'd been strangely quiet for much of the afternoon. "You okay?" she asked.

"Me?" he looked at her. "I'm fine. Why?"

"Well, you haven't said much. I thought maybe you were mad at me or something."

"No. Nothing's wrong."

That's what he said, but he wasn't smiling. Something was definitely wrong. Pekin sighed.

TAKING TWO STEPS AT A TIME, Pekin raced to her room. She couldn't wait to look at the pictures of Miranda again. In a rush, she slammed her door, jumped on her bed, and pulled out her phone.

"What?" Pekin scrolled through the pictures. If she squinted, she could see a vague outline where Miranda had stood, but it was obvious the ghost was fading away. *Oh, no,* she thought. *Scout and Amber are going to be so disappointed. They wanted copies of the pictures.*

She texted the pictures to her friends, with a note about the missing ghost.

Amber texted right back. *How can that be?*

I don't know. So far, there's still a very faint outline of her. I hope that doesn't fade away.

I was going to show Josh. Now I can't.

You what?? You know we can't tell people. Pekin was livid.

God. I was just kidding. Our secret is safe with me.

Don't scare me like that. I mean, I couldn't be sure, what with your vitally important date coming up. It could happen.

Ha ha. I'm going now. I have to think about my vitally important date some more.

G'night, weirdo.

CHAPTER TWENTY-ONE

ON PROM NIGHT, PEKIN'S DAD snapped photos as she came down the stairs.

"Honey, you're beautiful," her mother said, her eyes growing misty. "You look so grown up."

"My little girl's a young lady now," her father said with a slight tremor in his voice.

She shook her head. "Thanks, Daddy." She struck some Kardashian poses for the camera before a knock at the door signaled Allen had arrived.

"You look amazing," he said with a huge grin when he saw her.

"Thank you," she said shyly. "You look nice, too."

"You're so cute together," Melissa said, clasping her hands in front of her.

"Let me get some pictures of you two before you go," her dad said, posing them by the front door.

They waved goodbye and climbed into the front seat of Allen's car. Allen's parents' *blue minivan*, that is.

Really cool to drive up to the prom in that, Pekin thought, then kicked herself for being so shallow. She turned in her seat to say hi to Amber and Josh, smiling when she saw they were holding hands. She raised her eyebrow at Amber when Josh looked away for a moment, and Amber wiggled her eyebrows back with a big grin.

The high school gymnasium was blinged out with mirror balls and hanging crystal chandeliers. The DJ blared Avicii, Bon Jovi, Ke$ha and videos played on screens set around the gym. Pekin and Amber and their dates rushed to join the other kids on the dance floor. They didn't stop dancing until the DJ went on a break, then the boys went to fetch drinks while Pekin and Amber caught their breath.

"This is so fun," Amber gushed. "I can't wait for a slow dance."

"I can imagine."

"I think Josh likes me. I'm dying to dance slow with him."

Pekin grinned at her friend. She was enjoying dancing with Allen, but she hoped he could tell she didn't see him as anything more than a friend.

The break was long enough that they were excited when the music started up again. The third song was a slow one. Pekin watched Amber's face assume a dreamy expression as she moved into Josh's arms, and Pekin winked at her.

Allen put his arms around her for the dance. She resisted his efforts to pull her close and maintained a comfortable distance. A second slow dance followed. This time she relaxed into his arms a little, feeling guilty as she pretended it was Scout holding her. She closed her eyes and let the music carry her. When she opened them, Vanessa Dooley was standing at the edge of the dance floor, sparkling like a princess in the glittering lights of the mirror ball. Vanessa Dooley in a form-fitting emerald green dress. Vanessa Dooley, smiling up at...Scout.

Pekin's heart sank to her feet and she gulped to stop the tears forming behind her eyes. She mumbled an apology and pulled away from Allen, who stood on the dance floor looking confused as she hurried away.

Pekin couldn't resist looking back, and she couldn't miss Scout watching her, as Vanessa Dooley pulled him onto the dance floor. Pekin made a beeline for the girl's bathroom and locked herself in one of the stalls. It took a few minutes for her to gain control over her emotions. She leaned against the door, trying to slow her breathing and calm the pounding of her heart.

With a deep breath, she knew what she had to do. She examined her reflection in the mirror for signs of the emotional trauma she'd endured. Confident no one would be able to tell how near she'd come to dissolving in a puddle of tears, she arranged her hair to fall in a flattering manner around her face, then squared her shoulders and exited the bathroom.

Allen was sitting at their table, and she leaned over his shoulder apologizing for running off, then asked if he'd like to try again. He smiled tentatively and stood, taking her hand and leading her back onto the dance floor.

She purposely didn't look at Scout as he and Vanessa Dooley danced three couples away. Instead, she focused her attention on Allen, gazing up into his eyes and smiling a big, happy, painfully fake smile.

It seemed perfect when Taylor Swift's "You Belong with Me" began to play, and Pekin moved into Allen's arms. Scout would see Pekin falling for Allen. Vanessa Dooley could have him.

Pekin really worked it. Her arms went around Allen's neck and she playfully smiled up at him the way she'd seen Vanessa Dooley gaze up at Scout. The plan seemed to be working until Allen misread, or maybe he didn't realize he was part of a con, and he bent close and kissed her.

It took her by surprise. She let slip a little "Oh," and pulled back. When she noticed Scout watching, she snuggled back into Allen's arms and gave him a 50-watt coy smile. Secretly, she wished the evening was over.

When the dance ended, Allen took Pekin's hand to lead her back to their table. Her eyes scanned the dance floor, but Scout and Vanessa Dooley weren't there. And she didn't spot them upon further scrutiny of the gym.

Before she could process her feelings of disappointment, a glowing, bubbly Amber grabbed her arm and dragged her off to the girl's bathroom with an apology directed at Allen. The door had barely closed behind them when Amber launched into an excited recounting of the magic moment Josh had told her he liked her. "And he kissed me," she blushed.

Pekin's heart clenched when she thought about *her* first kiss. With Allen. She'd hoped her first kiss would be with Scout. But it wouldn't do to be a wet blanket on her best friend's happiness, so Pekin hugged Amber and made appropriately excited, supportive comments.

Amber went with it and continued her gushing joy, until she stopped to breathe. That's when she noticed Pekin's face.

"Spill. What's wrong?" Amber asked. "And don't say 'nothing,' because I can see you're upset about something."

Pekin sighed. Her eyes filled with the tears she'd tried to hold back.

"Oh, Pekie. What is it?" Amber grabbed Pekin's shoulders and looked into her eyes.

Pekin glanced down but she could feel Amber's relentless gaze and knew she had to *spill*.

"Did you see Scout?"

"He's here?"

"Yes. With Vanessa Dooley."

Amber looked stricken. "Oh, Pekie. I'm so sorry. Do you want to leave?"

"That wouldn't be fair to you. I know you want to be with Josh."

"I do, but now that he said he likes me, I'm sure I'll be seeing more of him. But I don't want you to—"

"No. I'm okay. I'm not sure he and Vanessa Dooley are still here. I didn't see them after...after...well, after Allen kissed me."

"Allen kissed you?"

"Yes, but I wanted my first kiss to be with Scout," she said, turning to the mirror. "I have to freshen up. Allen's going to wonder where I went." Pekin grabbed a paper towel and carefully wiped at her eyes. She straightened up and looked appraisingly at her reflection. "Do I look like I've been crying?"

"Only to me. Allen will never know." She put her arm around Pekin's shoulders and said, "I'm sorry."

Pekin shrugged. "I'll get over it. Let's go get through the rest of this night."

PEKIN SILENTLY GAZED OUT THE WINDOW on the ride home, wishing she was already there.

Amber chattered happily in the back seat, Josh's arm slung possessively over her shoulders. The night had certainly turned out well for her, Pekin thought, glad for her friend.

"Do you mind dropping me off first?" Pekin asked Allen. "My feet hurt and I can't wait to get in my pajamas."

"I thought maybe we could stop for a Starbucks or something," he said, sounding disappointed.

"Maybe some other time. You guys go, though. I'm tired." Feeling guilty, she added, "We danced our feet off tonight, didn't we? It was fun. Thanks for asking me, Allen."

He smiled a half smile as he pulled up to her house. He opened her door and walked her up to the front door. He awkwardly waited as she dug her key out of her clutch, but when he leaned in for a kiss, she offered her cheek instead and said goodnight.

"Maybe we can get together again," he said hopefully as she pushed open the door.

"We'll see," she said. "Thanks again for tonight." She smiled at him before disappearing into the safety of her house.

RETREATING UNDER HER COMFORTER, she pulled out her phone and texted Scout. *Hey, where'd you go? I looked all over for you. I wanted to say hi.* She knew it was the last thing she should do, but she couldn't stop herself.

She didn't get a response.

Thoughts of Scout ran through her head as she dropped off to sleep. Was he jealous? *Of course not. He has Vanessa Dooley to help him get over anything he needs to get over.*

Monday morning, Pekin was too sad to get out of bed. She hadn't been able to get the image of Scout dancing with Vanessa Dooley out of her head since prom. The way she tossed her hair and smiled up into his eyes. Her hand on the back of his neck, touching his hair. She'd probably kissed him, too. Whatever farfetched idea Pekin had that maybe Scout might like her back, seeing him with Vanessa Dooley had spiked it right out of her brain. She rolled over and curled into a ball, pulling the covers over her head, until the third time the snooze alarm went off and she had to drag herself out of bed and into the bathroom. She took a few deep breaths as she gazed into the mirror to shake off the gloomy thoughts that had plagued her all night long. By the time she was out of the shower, though, Pekin felt ready to face the day. And Scout.

Scout's locker was near hers, but when she stopped to get her books before her first class, she didn't see him at his locker. This left her all morning to stew about what would happen at lunch. Assuming he'd still have lunch with her and Amber instead of Vanessa Dooley.

She spotted him with Amber in the quad. He looked away when she joined them.

"Why didn't you text me back last night? I was worried about you."

"I don't know why you would be," he said, his voice stiff and impersonal. "As you can see, I'm fine."

"Where did you and Vanessa Dooley disappear to?" Pekin asked, even though she wasn't sure she wanted to hear the answer.

He smirked and rolled his eyes, but didn't answer.

She looked at him sharply. "Are you mad at me or something?"

He sniffed condescendingly. "Why would I be mad at you?"

"I don't know. That's why I'm asking."

"Nope. Everything's fine," he said, but Pekin didn't buy it.

Amber watched the back and forth conversation as the three of them went through the lunch line and carried their food to a table. Pekin was relieved when Amber diplomatically refrained from asking Scout about Vanessa Dooley, instead expounding on her fabulous time with Josh. She laughed gaily during her tale, but it wasn't enough to jolly her friends out of the uneasy truce they'd seemingly fallen into.

Lunch went fast, as no one seemed to be comfortable. Even Scout only picked at the pizza he normally wolfed down.

Pekin stood and opened her mouth to speak just as Allen walked up. "Hello, ladies, Scout. Saturday night was fun. I had a great time, Pekin."

Her stomach sank. Just what she wanted to deal with. She forced a smile. "Yes. I had fun, too."

"Do you have any big plans this summer?" Allen asked. "Maybe we could hang out sometime?"

"Oh, sure. I suppose we could," she replied, distracted.

Scout made a face, mumbled something about a class, then turned and left.

"What was *that* about?" Amber asked.

"I don't know. He's mad at me and I don't know what I did."

The last thing she felt like doing was dealing with Allen. She was absorbed with Scout's behavior. She'd be lucky if she could pay any attention in class. Thankfully, it was her last one so she could go home and brood afterward.

"Nice to see you, Allen. I've got to get to class. I'll talk to you later."

Amber left with her, leaving Allen standing alone, watching them walk away.

Pekin texted Amber once she got to class. *You know we're supposed to go back to Elmwood Manor. What if Scout doesn't want to go?*

You're jumping to conclusions. I'm sure he'll be there. He knows it's important.

Yeah, well. You're not the one he's mad at.

I'm not sure mad *is the right word. If you ask me, he acted jealous.*

Jealous? Scout doesn't think of me that way.

He saw you kissing Allen. That could make him jealous.

He doesn't care. He was with Vanessa Dooley. I can't compete with her.

Are we back to this? Do I really need to go back through the list of why you're the better match for Scout?

Thanks, but I don't think...

Don't think. Whatever's bothering him, he'll get over it.

Pekin didn't text her back. She was too busy stubbornly thinking about all the ways Amber was probably wrong.

Chapter Twenty-Two

TOSSING AND TURNING, Pekin's fitful sleep was interrupted by dreams of Scout holding her in his arms as they danced at the prom. In snatches and bits, his face swirled around her, interspersed with scenes of the dusty hallways and creaky stairs of Elmwood Manor.

She woke up depressed. It had almost seemed real, being with Scout. She sighed as she swung her legs off the bed and stretched. This wasn't the way the first day of summer break should be starting out.

Having a naturally sunny disposition, by the time she'd brushed her teeth and showered, she was back to her normal cheerful self. Scout was one of her best friends. No matter what was bugging him, he'd be back.

She was nervous when she texted him and Amber about Monday. What if he didn't respond? What was she supposed to do then?

Amber responded right away *What time?*

She texted back, *ten?*

Then she texted *Scout?*

She was starting to slip back into anxiety when her phone dinged with a text from Scout. *Ten is fine. I'll pick you guys up.*

Pekin could breathe again. Whatever was bugging him, at least they'd be spending the day together on Monday and she'd pry the truth out of him.

Chapter Twenty-Three

A T ELMWOOD ON MONDAY, Amber kept gushing about her date with Josh on Saturday night. Apparently, they were a *thing*.

"Have you heard from Allen?" she asked. "He wants to get together with you over the summer."

Pekin squirmed on the parlor sofa, causing a small cloud of dust to dance around her bottom. "No. I haven't heard from him." She glanced at Scout, who quickly looked away, then bent to go through his backpack.

"So, you went to the prom with Vanessa, Scout?" Amber kept up her not-so-clueless chatter. "Pekin said she saw you."

"We were there for a while."

"Why didn't you find us to say hi?" Amber prodded.

"You guys, we need to talk to Miranda," Pekin said, not wanting to continue talking about the prom. "Can we concentrate on why we're here?"

"Yes. Let's," Scout said.

Pekin glanced at him, but he wouldn't meet her gaze, so she pulled *Harry Potter* out of her backpack and sat down. "Miranda, are you here?

"We need to talk to her," Scout said. "We can't *play* with her every time we come over here."

"I know," Pekin said. "But I don't want to push her."

"It feels like stalling to me," he said.

"You're being weird," Pekin retorted, an edge to her voice.

He shrugged. "Do what you want."

"Let's play some music," Amber said. "She likes dancing."

"Is that too boring for you, Scout?" Pekin said. "I don't want you to feel like you're wasting your time."

Amber shot her a look. "What's wrong with you guys? Why don't you two patch it up so we can get on with it?"

Scout grunted. He'd pulled his phone out and buried his nose in it.

Pekin scowled at him. "There's nothing to patch up. Nothing's wrong."

"If you say so," Amber said.

The temperature dropped. Even Scout looked up.

"Miranda?" Pekin asked.

Yes, came a voice. Miranda's familiar shimmer appeared in the doorway to the hall. She was clearer now, more solid. Maybe the energy from the kids enabled her to be more fully present.

"Hi," Amber said.

Hello, Miranda responded.

An uncomfortable silence fell over the room, and Miranda looked from one to another questioningly.

"So, what do we do now?" Scout said, putting into words a question they all felt.

"What Scout *means,*" Pekin said, shooting him a look, "is that we don't know what you might like to do. I mean, do you like the music, or do you want me to read to you?"

"Pekin," Scout said. "We should talk to her. We're wasting time."

She glared at him, but turned to the ghost. "Miranda, we need to talk to you about something. We don't want you to be mad or scared. All we want to do is help you. Will you hear us out?"

Miranda nodded, but said nothing.

"You've been in this house for a very long time. Over a hundred years. We want to help you move on. You know, go to heaven, be with your parents. To do that, we have to find out what happened to you way back when you...you died."

Miranda's face reflected her unease, and Pekin was concerned she'd vanish. She glanced at Amber for help.

"Only if you want to, though," Amber said. "If you want to stay here, of course you can. But it must be so lonely being here by yourself for all this time."

I am not alone, Miranda said with surprising force. *There's—.*

A knock at the door caused her to disappear. Amber, Pekin and Scout looked at each other. "Are we expecting your mom or anyone?"

Amber asked.

"No," Pekin answered as she opened the door.

Her mouth fell open when she saw the tiny round woman standing on the stoop.

"*You*," Pekin said. "Who are you and what do you want?"

Scout joined her. "Who is it?"

"I don't know, but I've seen her watching this house more than once." She returned her attention to the woman. "Who are you?"

"I'm sorry to barge in on you like this—"

"Then why did you?" Pekin wasn't usually rude, but the surprise visit had shaken her up. "You've been watching us."

"Not you. Not exactly you. I was interested in this house, and then I saw you young people coming and going."

"So what?" Pekin asked. "It's not your house."

"No, it's not my house. It hasn't been anybody's house for a very long time. In fact—"

"I don't know why you're here, but—"

"Pekin." Scout put a hand on her shoulder. "Why don't we see what she wants?"

Pekin opened her mouth to speak, but then nodded. "Okay, fine."

Amber peeked around Scout. "Should we invite her in?"

Scout shrugged. "Pekin?"

Against her better judgment, Pekin gave in. "Do you want to come in?" she asked the little woman.

"Yes. Thank you, dear."

She followed them into the parlor. Pekin turned to face the woman, her arms crossed over her chest. "Why have you been spying on us?"

"I assure you, I haven't been spying on you." The small woman set her handbag down on the library table, then extended her hand. "I'm Mildred Willingham. You may call me Mildew. Everyone does." When Pekin didn't take her hand, Scout did.

"I'm Scout, that's Amber, and your friend here is Pekin."

Pekin shot him another look.

"Thank you, Scout. I simply had to speak with you all. Growing up, I heard lots of stories of strange happenings here. My curiosity became more intense over time. My dreams and clairvoyance pulled me to this house. Driven by a premonition that something in this place is coming to a head, I've felt a pull to the house in a way I haven't experienced before. I'm not sure if you know this, but I believe this house is haunted."

Once again Pekin's mouth fell open.

"We know," offered Amber. "But what does that have to do with you?"

Mildew sighed. "Ever since I was a child, I've been able to see people who've passed on. Spirits seek me out because I help them to leave this plane behind and cross over to the other side."

"But why are you here?" Pekin asked. "What does that have to do with anything?"

"As I said, I've been drawn here. Someone here needs my help."

"If anyone here needs help, we'll take care of it," Pekin said.

"Admirable, dear, but do you know how?"

Pekin didn't answer.

"Pekin?" Amber said.

"Of course we do." She couldn't help noticing Amber's shocked face. "Thank you for checking up on us, Ms. Wilbertson, but we're fine."

"It's Willingham, dear," Mildew said. "I don't want to step on any toes, but wanted to offer my help. Or advice. If you should find that you need anything," she dug in her bag, "here's my card. Please call me." She smiled tentatively at the group, then turned and left.

"*Pekin*. She knows stuff. Why did you send her away?" Amber asked.

"We don't know her. What if she wants to steal our business for herself?"

"I didn't get that from her," Scout said. "She seemed sincere."

"Just because she said all that doesn't mean it's true. Besides, we don't know that we need any help. We haven't even tried yet. Look how far we've gotten so far. Miranda knows us. She trusts us."

Amber took the business card out of Pekin's hand. "I'll hold onto this, just in case."

"Miranda?" Pekin called but got no response. She felt sure Miranda wouldn't come out again. At least, not today. There was too much tension in the room.

She picked up her backpack. "Shall we call it a day? We can try again tomorrow. We'll get right down to business and tell her what we're doing."

"Fine with me," Scout said.

"Me, too," Amber added.

On the way home, Amber scrolled through her phone. She held it up to Pekin. "Look, Pekie, Mildew has a Wikipedia page."

"So?"

"So, here. Let me see what it says about her. She saw her first ghost when she was 6. Like you, Pekin."

"I was 5."

"Yeah, I can see how that would erase anything she has in common with you." Amber rolled her eyes. "At age 12, when her mother realized Mildew really did see ghosts, she took her daughter to a woman in town people went to in order to communicate with their departed loved ones. She began training with the woman and learned how to help the spirits cross over. Wait, it says here that she's worked with police departments to find missing people and solve cold cases." She glanced at Pekin. "That's pretty impressive, don't you think?"

She looked at her phone again. "And it says she's a psychic. Isn't that cool?"

"Why are you so bonkers over that woman?" Pekin asked, scowling over her shoulder at her friend.

"I think we should consider calling her if we need to," Scout said.

"Fine. Keep her number handy. If you think I can't handle the job."

"It has nothing to do with that. I'm sure you can handle it. Probably. But, if we should need help, it's good to know there's someone we could call," Scout said, ever the reasonable one. "Why are you so agitated about Mildew?" Scout asked. "Do you feel threatened or something?"

Pekin scowled some more, then seemed to relax. "I don't know. I guess I'm all nervous about our big talk with Miranda, and then that woman comes in the middle of it. I'm sure she's perfectly nice, but she's been spying on us, and I don't like it."

"What do you mean spying on us?" Amber asked.

"I've seen her watching the house. Once she was standing on the sidewalk, and the other time in her car. When she saw me looking at her, she burned rubber leaving the scene."

"I guess that's strange," Amber said. "Anyway, tomorrow should be interesting. I mean, when we talk to Miranda again. I'm kinda nervous, too."

"Get a good night's sleep, then," Pekin said. "So you'll be ready for the big talk."

Scout pulled up to the curb to let Amber out of the car.

Pekin watched her walk up to the front door, nervous at being left alone with Scout. Her palms were sweaty and she swallowed to calm the butterflies in her stomach. She didn't turn from the window as the car sped up.

"I want to go back," she finally said.

He looked at her. "Back where? To Elmwood?"

"Yes. When it gets dark."

"You've got to be kidding."

She turned on him. "I'm not. Since it's obvious you don't want to go with me, I'll go by myself."

He didn't say anything as he pulled up in front of her house. She didn't say anything as she got out of the car and stalked up her front walk. At the door, she turned and walked back to the car. Leaning down, she said through the window, "Since you're obviously mad at me, can you at least try to be civil? We have to save Miranda. Unless you're planning to ditch us."

He shook his head in exasperation. "First of all, I'm not ditching you. And I'll be as civil as you are."

"Hmpf," she grunted. "I notice you didn't say you're not mad." She stood and walked back to her front door before he could answer. She didn't look back as she pushed open the door and disappeared inside.

Chapter Twenty-Four

IT WAS RAINING THE NEXT DAY when they made the trip to Elmwood Manor. The sound of water rushing past in the gutter seemed to enhance the dreary mood. They stashed their boots and umbrellas by the front door, and shuffled anxiously into the parlor.

Pekin stole a quick glance at Scout, to find him watching her. She started, then squared her shoulders. "Are we good?" she asked, working to keep a harsh tone out of her voice.

He nodded and looked away.

Pekin took her usual seat on the sofa. "We're back, Miranda. Can you come out? We didn't know that person would show up yesterday and scare you away. It's just us today."

Nothing.

"Please, Miranda. It's important." Pekin said. "For you and for us."

"Miranda," Scout added. "Give us a chance to explain what we're trying to do here. It can't hurt to hear us out. The final decision is yours. We're your friends and want to help in any way we can." He looked at Pekin and shrugged.

Scout saw the shimmer first and pointed.

As the shimmer became the girl, it floated to the sofa and sat. Miranda looked troubled.

Amber sat beside her. "Why are you sad?"

Because you don't understand.

"What don't we understand?"

I can't leave this house. Ever.

"Why?" Pekin asked.

Because I'm lost.

"We know. We want to help find you. Do you remember your last day?"

Miranda looked away silently.

"Can you tell us what happened to you?" Scout asked.

"If you don't tell us, no one will ever know. That's not a good thing," Pekin said.

Miranda picked at the skirt of her dress, then smoothed it out. *I was fourteen.* The ghost sighed. *I don't like to look back.*

"I'd hold your hand if I could," Amber said. "You're safe with us."

"Why don't you start at the beginning," Pekin said. "That might be easiest for you."

Miranda seemed to shrink in on herself, her shoulders slumping, her head bent. She spoke without lifting her head. *It was April 14, 1918. After church, our maid prepared brunch, and we spent the afternoon in our individual pursuits. My cousin Nyla and I read in the parlor until it was time for her to go. I watched from the window as Nyla and my aunt and uncle left. My parents stood on the porch to wave them off. I heard a noise behind me and someone grabbed me. They covered my mouth so I couldn't scream.* Shimmering ghost tears slipped from Miranda's eyes and she took several deep breaths. *He rushed through the house with me and out the back door. I kicked at him and he let out a groan. He let go of my mouth and hit me. When I awoke, it was dark and there was dirt and the ground was hard as he pushed me down. He reached up to cover my mouth and I bit his finger hard. I bit it off.*

Pekin stared wide-eyed. "You did?"

And I swallowed it.

"Ewww!" Amber shuddered. "Why?"

Because I didn't want him to be able to get it back.

"Good," Scout said under his breath.

He was so furious, he hit me. His hands went around my neck and he shook me. He was kneeling on my chest. I couldn't breathe. He was screaming at me and calling me a bad name. He banged my head against the ground again and again and squeezed my neck hard. I tried to fight. I did. But my vision began to fade and my head hurt terribly. I couldn't scream because he held my throat so tight. And then it was done.

"It was done?" Amber asked in horror.

Yes. It was done. I knew nothing more, until I woke up and no one could see me anymore.

Pekin let out the breath she'd been holding as she listened to the story.

"That bastard," Scout said.

"Where? Do you know where you were?" Pekin asked. "We need to find you."

Miranda shook her head. *It was so dark. I could only fight.*

"Do you know who it was?"

Yes, but I mustn't say.

Scout knelt in front of her. "Miranda, you have to tell us."

"We want to help you leave this place," Amber said. "You must be so tired of being alone here."

Miranda stood suddenly. *I am not alone.*

A door slammed upstairs. They all jumped.

Please, help me, Miranda begged as the lights flickered.

"We will," Amber said. Miranda shimmered and vanished. Something fell to the floor in front of Amber. Looking down, Amber saw a small key on a tattered white ribbon. She bent to pick it up.

The doors upstairs slammed one after another. **Get out.** The voice was deep and menacing. They heard heavy footsteps approaching the top of the stairs. In a panic, they grabbed their gear and fled the house.

Chapter Twenty-Five

~~~~~~

T HEY STOOD IN THE FRONT YARD looking back, none of them
saying anything for a moment.

"Let's get out of here," Amber said, breaking the silence.
They scrambled into Scout's car and he screeched away from the curb.

"What the *hell?*" Scout said. "What the hell was that?"

"More like, *who* was that?" Pekin said.

"Miranda said she wasn't alone here. Maybe—"

"Did someone else die in this house?" Scout asked.

"It's been a hundred years since Miranda was killed. It's possible
someone else could have—" Pekin started.

"Died there? Wouldn't Elonia have known about it? Besides, she
said the house has mostly been empty for years because of the haunting.
Maybe we should Google it."

"I *have* Googled Elmwood," Pekin said. "I didn't find anything
about another death."

Amber suddenly remembered the key, and she opened her hand
and offered it to Pekin. "What do you think this is for?"

"Oh," Pekin said in surprise. "Where did—"

"Miranda. I think she wanted to hand it to me but couldn't, so she
dropped it on the floor at my feet."

Pekin turned it over and examined it. It was too small for a house
key, and different than the key to the rolltop desk.

"Maybe a diary?" Pekin mused.

"It must be important for Miranda to give it to you," Scout said.
"We need to figure it out."

"Do we want to go back there?" Amber said.

"She needs our help," Pekin said. "If she's in danger there, we
really need to go back."

"I agree with Pekin," Scout said. "Look, we'll all stick together. We should be okay."

"I think we should sneak back in and be silent. Maybe we'll be able to find out who the scary voice is."

"You mean now?" Amber asked.

"No. Tonight," Pekin said.

"I'm not going in that house at night," Amber said.

"I don't think it's a good idea either," Scout added.

"Okay," Pekin said as if she didn't care.

"I think she's giving up too easily," Scout said.

"As long as she gives up, it's okay with me," Amber said.

Pekin didn't respond. When the car pulled up in front of Amber's house, Pekin waved goodbye and said she'd see her tomorrow.

"You're not seriously going to try to go there tonight, are you?" Scout asked.

"Don't worry about it," Pekin said. "*You* don't have to be there so it's not your business."

"You're being a little mean there, Pekie."

"Says the person who's barely talked to me for days. So, again, don't worry about it."

Scout pulled up to the curb in front of the Dewlap house. "Pekin, I—"

She yanked open the car door and scooted out. She pasted a smile on her face and said, "See you tomorrow." An instant later, she was closing the front door, leaving Scout frowning.

PEKIN CHANGED INTO JEANS and a hoodie. She tiptoed out into the hall and listened. The sounds of *Modern Family* reruns floated up from the family room. Picking up her backpack, she carefully made her way downstairs and out the kitchen door to the garage. Using the flashlight on her phone, she found her bicycle mounted on a rack. She moved slowly to make as little noise as possible, lifting the bike from its holder and carefully opening the side door. The sound of the garage door opening would have alerted her parents that someone was in the garage. She didn't want to take the chance. The side door led into the side yard where she silently unlatched the gate. Then she was on her way.

Ten o'clock at night and it was still over 80 degrees outside, and humid from the rain. By the time she reached Elmwood, which was a grueling twenty-minute ride, she felt like she was draped in blankets. She'd ditch the hoodie when she got into the house.

Pekin leaned her bike against the side of the house, pulling the flashlight out of her backpack as she walked around to the front door. She snapped the flashlight on as she eased through the door, moving as stealthy as possible. It was dark in the parlor, with only the pale moonlight streaming in the windows to illuminate the furnishings, which seemed sinister in the dark shadows.

She didn't want to turn on the lights, hoping to observe without being detected. It was warmer in the parlor than she would have liked. *Why should I have expected this to be a pleasant experience?* she asked herself.

There were some things Pekin hadn't factored into her plan. It would be difficult to read without any lights on. She couldn't listen to music without alerting the other spirit to her presence, and if she used earbuds she wouldn't be able to hear, assuming there was something to hear. Thank goodness she had her phone.

When she'd imagined her night in the haunted house, she pictured herself curling up on the sofa with a nice romance novel. A scary book would have been a bad idea, given the circumstances. From her backpack, which rested against the end of the sofa, she removed a bottle of water.

She scooted into one corner of the sofa and pulled her legs up under her, and sat waiting to see what would happen.

Her nerves on edge, she tried to pretend she wasn't afraid, but it was so eerily quiet. At first. And dark. She became aware of the old house's creaks and groans, her heart racing with every sound as she tried to reassure herself that all old houses made noises as they settled.

Pekin was uncomfortable, and dismayed at how slowly the time was passing. A century of dust still coated much of the interior of Elmwood, despite the minimal cleaning they'd done to make the house more inviting. The dust hadn't been as obvious when they were active or visiting with Miranda, but sitting alone in the semi-dark of the parlor, the dust felt suffocating. And it was so hot. She used the paperback she'd brought to fan herself, and mopped at her sweaty forehead with paper towels from a roll that was left in a corner of the room. What she wouldn't do for a fan. The early summer heat in a closed-up house was oppressive.

The flashlight beam didn't offer comfort in the near pitch black parlor. Instead, it created eerie objects that were merely furniture in the daytime. Sitting in the dark, she second-guessed her decision to sneak back to the haunted house by herself. And she had time to analyze her motive. Maybe it didn't have as much to do with Miranda as it did with Scout. She knew he didn't think she should be here alone. She hoped he was worried that she might actually do it and show up to be with her. But chances were his thoughts were on Vanessa Dooley. Pekin was so mad at him. She felt like he was betraying her, which she knew was unfair, but she couldn't help feeling cheated. She couldn't help being mad at him.

It was midnight, and Pekin had successfully lasted two hours. So far it had been a bust. She wasn't sure what she'd hoped would happen, but a big nothing wasn't it.

Then she heard what sounded like a ball bouncing upstairs. After debating with herself, Pekin beat back her fear of the unknown and started for the stairs, hoping it was Miranda entertaining herself in her room.

At the top of the stairs, she could tell the sound was indeed coming from Miranda's room. Pekin tiptoed down the long hallway toward the bedroom.

The door was open and Pekin took a deep breath, hoping to quiet her loudly beating heart before she poked her head in the doorway. The room was empty and the noise had stopped. She realized she probably shouldn't have left her phone downstairs.

"Miranda," Pekin whispered, stepping inside. She whispered again, a little louder, but there was no answer. She stepped backward, but was pushed from behind. The door slammed shut, plunging her into darkness. Landing on her hands and knees, the flashlight went flying off into the distance. She was too scared to feel any pain where her knees had been skinned raw from hitting the hardwood floor. She crawled around, searching for the flashlight.

Tears of frustration welled up in her eyes when she couldn't find it. Her heart caught in her throat when she realized the only place it could be was under the bed. *Under the bed.*

Maybe she should leave it there. After a moment's debate, she scolded herself for being afraid and lifted up the brittle, fragile bed skirt and reached her arm underneath. She felt around and breathed a sigh of relief when her hand closed around the flashlight. Before she could pull it out, something grabbed her arm and yanked her toward the blackness waiting under the bed.

Pekin let out a bloodcurdling scream and jerked back on her arm, pulling it free of whatever had tried to drag her to a place she was too horrified to imagine.

She scrambled backward on her rear end until she felt the door behind her. Jumping to her feet, she grabbed the doorknob. It twisted uselessly in her hand. She was trapped. She pounded on the door, calling for help she was certain would never come. She cried as she thought about how they'd find her cold dead body in the morning. Her ghost would wander the halls of Elmwood with Miranda and the thing under the bed.

Sliding down until she was sitting against the door, she alternated between yelling for help and sobbing.

A sound came from the direction of the bed, like something heavy being drug out from under. Or was crawling out from under. And scary, scary laughter. She covered her face with her hands and prepared to die as something cold wrapped around her ankle and started to pull her across the floor.

She whimpered as she saw the dim shape of the bed looming larger, then kicked hard with her foot and screamed, "Let me go!"

She twisted and rolled over onto her stomach, her legs tangled as the thing kept hold of her. It pulled her toward the yawning black hole waiting for her under the bed. Adrenaline surged through her as she fought for her life, giving her the energy to flail and kick and screech. All hope fled as she felt the bed skirt brushing against her legs as they were swallowed by the darkness.

The bedroom door flew open. "*Pekin!*" Scout sounded frantic as his strong arms gripped her and tugged, yanking her free of whatever had her in its clutches.

"Scout. Oh, Scout." Pekin clung to him, her breath rasping in her chest and tears coursing down her cheeks.

His arm protectively wrapped around her waist, he pulled her from the room, and the two of them sprinted down the hallway and down the stairs as a deep growl rumbled behind them. Pekin pointed to the parlor. Scout nodded as she detoured into the room to grab her backpack and phone. Then both of them were out the front door, not stopping until they crossed the sidewalk and stood safely by Scout's car.

Pekin wiped briskly at her eyes, and used the bottom of her shirt to dry them. But the tears came back full force. She melted into Scout's arms. He cradled her protectively, holding her tight, smothering her in his big arms.

When her trembling stopped, he loosened his hold, then held her at arm's length and looked at her.

"Are you okay?" he asked.

"You saved me! Oh, Scout. I was so *scared*."

"What happened in there?"

"It locked me in Miranda's room. It tried to pull me *under the bed*." Her voice went up at the end and Scout put his arms around her again.

"Was it Miranda?"

"I don't know what it was. I'm sure it wasn't Miranda. She wouldn't do that to me."

He looked doubtful, but didn't argue. Instead, he held her at arm's length again and scowled at her sternly. "What were you thinking going there alone at night?"

She shook free of his hands and glared back. "I told you I thought we needed to go there at night. You didn't want to go with me, so I went by myself."

"We never really discussed it. I didn't know you were serious."

"Then why are you here?"

"Because. Because I was afraid you might really do something stupid like that. I had a feeling. I couldn't sleep, so I took a chance and drove by here. And what do I see? Your blue bicycle leaning against the side of the house." He crossed his arms. "I guess it's a good thing I did."

"Yes, it was a good thing you did," she said softly, thankful for his strong arms.

Chapter Twenty-Six

~~~~~~

PEKIN SNUCK BACK INTO HER HOUSE and to bed shortly after one. She curled on her side, pulling her green cotton duvet up around her neck, struggling with shutting out the events of the night enough to fall asleep. Griselda pushed open the not-quite-closed bedroom door and positioned herself on the pillow, resting against Pekin's head. She took a small nip at Pekin's ear, as if to say *where were you?*

"I'm sorry, sweetie," Pekin said, rubbing the little gray and white head before tucking her hand back under the covers.

She tossed and turned fitfully, her dreams morphing into nightmares of running up and down the hallways of Elmwood as something big and dark gained on her. Her dreams mingled with the memory of Scout coming to her rescue. The way he swept in and saved her life. Her dreams and memory mingled with sadness that Scout was with Vanessa Dooley, and she slipped back into sleep as tears dampened her pillow.

Around 5:00 a.m., Pekin's eyes flew open. She knew what the key was for. She wanted to call Amber, but it was *way* too early, so she contented herself with knowing they had somewhere to search for clues.

Morning couldn't come soon enough for Pekin. She was out of bed by 7:30 and ready to go by 8:30. It seemed an eternity before she heard Scout honk.

"You look *great*," he said with more than a touch of sarcasm. "I think raccoon eyes are in this season."

She batted her eyes at him and said, "Thanks." She was too euphoric over her discovery to be offended.

"How are you?" His eyes reflected his concern.

"Oh, you know. I'm okay."

"Are you sure you want to go back there?" he asked.

Pekin took a deep breath. "Yes, I want to go back."

"I thought you'd have had enough of that place after last night."

"I was scared and had nightmares all night. But, Scout, we have to finish what we started." She looked at him, willing him to understand. "We won't...*I* won't...go back there at night, but we can't give up now. Miranda could be in danger."

He nodded, but didn't say anything. They rode in silence the rest of the way to Amber's house.

Pekin had a cheery "Hi" for Amber when they picked her up at the curb in front of her house. She ignored the pointed looks Scout kept shooting her way for the rest of the drive to Elmwood.

Pekin opened the door and glanced around nervously before stepping inside, followed by Scout and Amber.

"Are you going to tell Amber what you did last night?" Scout asked as he dropped his backpack on the floor by the front door.

"I have something to tell Amber, and you, that's *way* more important."

"Wait, what did you do last night?" Amber asked.

"She rode her bike over here and sat around in a dark house. Then she got locked in Miranda's room with a monster under the bed. I had to practically break the door down to rescue her."

"My hero," Pekin said. "But I'm fine. See?"

"How could you *do* that?" Amber's face turned pale and she shuddered.

"I wanted to see what was scaring Miranda."

"If something scares an actual ghost, doesn't it follow that it would scare you a hundred times more?" Amber's eyes were as big as an anime cat's.

"I think she was trying to make a point," Scout said.

Pekin glared at him.

"About what?" Amber asked.

"How brave she was. Or," he paused to glare at Pekin, "she wanted to piss me off."

"You're already pissed off at me."

"God, you guys. You haven't patched things up yet?"

"I don't even know why he's mad at me," Pekin said, frowning. "Besides, there's more important stuff to talk about. The key. It's for the cedar chest. It dawned on me early this morning. The chest we saw the first day we were in the attic. There must be something in it that can help us."

"Should we tell Miranda we're here?" Scout asked.

"I'm almost afraid to. Maybe if we're quiet, the other presence won't hear us."

"I think we should call her," Amber said.

Pekin looked at her. Amber was the most unlikely of them all to be the brave one. She smiled. "Way to go, Amber."

"What did I do?"

"You didn't chicken out. You stepped up."

"Oh, please. Give me a break."

Scout and Pekin laughed, their nerves gone for a brief moment.

"Come on. Let's go to the attic and check out the cedar chest," Pekin said. "She'll find us."

Nothing seemed out of place on the second floor, so they climbed the stairs to the attic. The creaking sound the door made when Pekin pushed it open momentarily scared her, but she covered her anxiety by grimacing over her shoulder at her friends in a comical way.

The sun shining through the dirty window gave the only light as dust motes danced in the beam. Pekin tried not to think about the fact that in the murky room the shrouded furniture seemed to conceal crouching monsters, but she couldn't help thinking of the one that had tried to pull her under the bed in Miranda's room. She straightened her shoulders and marched straight to the chest. Amber kept a wary watch while Pekin unlocked it. When she lifted the lid, they all crowded around to see what was inside.

A slightly discolored white lace dress was folded on top; small pink knitted booties and matching sweater and a sterling silver baby rattle underneath it barely concealed a leather-bound scrapbook. Pekin started to pull it out of the chest when Amber asked, "Do we have look through it here?"

"Yeah, let's take the chest downstairs where there's more light,"

Scout said.

Pekin lifted one corner to test its weight. "Can you carry it, Scout?" she asked, closing the lid. "It's heavy."

He grabbed the leather handles on each end of the chest and grunted as he heaved the box up.

"I can take one end if you want me to," Pekin said.

He shook his head. "No. Just make sure I don't trip on anything."

Pekin followed him down the stairs, holding onto the back belt-loop of his jeans to keep him from pitching down the stairs and breaking his neck.

He set the box down in the foyer and stepped back. Pekin knelt and opened the lid. "I think it's a wedding dress." She lifted the dress out and swirled around.

"Stop dancing with it," Amber cried, a note of hysteria in her voice. "This isn't fun and games."

As if to punctuate Amber's fear, Miranda shimmered into view on the bottom step of the stairs. *Please take the chest and go. He mustn't know you have it.* The ghost looked fearfully over her shoulder. *Hurry. Hurry and go.*

It took a moment for Pekin's surprise to wear off before she stuffed the dress back in the chest. "You heard her. Let's get out of here."

Amber snatched their backpacks and was first out the door. Scout and Pekin each took one handle and carried the chest outside.

"Thanks, Miranda," she called before she shut the door.

"Your house?" Scout asked Pekin as he put the Corolla in gear and pulled away from the curb.

"Yeah, my parents aren't home. We can order a pizza. I know that will make you happy."

When they reached her house, Pekin raced ahead to open the door as Scout muscled the trunk up the front walk and into the den.

"Okay, let's see what's in here," Pekin said.

She pulled out the dress, which brought with it a cloud of *eau de mothball*. "This lace is so intricate," Pekin said. "And still in pretty good shape. It probably belonged to Miranda's mother."

The baby items were fragile. Pekin was afraid to handle the baby sweater and booties, afraid the old yarn would fall to pieces if she touched it. Scout reached across her and picked up the silver rattle.

"Look," he said. "'MT' is engraved on it."

He handed it to Pekin. "It was Miranda's."

Pekin picked up the scrapbook, its leather cover cracked and powdery with age. When she opened it, the first item she saw was a folded note on fine cream stationery.

"What does it say?" Amber asked.

Pekin opened the note. Her eyes widened and she put her hand to her chest. "I think it's a note to Miranda from her mother."

Miranda, my angel,

It's been six years since we lost you. You would have been twenty years old today. So many birthdays I've missed with you. I pray every night that you'll come back to us, but in my heart I know it's not to be. I love you and miss you so much, my child. I cry myself to sleep at night. The hole in my heart will never close.

I love you,

Mother

No one spoke for several moments. "That's so sad," Amber said, wiping her eyes. "I feel so bad for her."

There were several yellowed and brittle news clippings of the crime. The Talberts hadn't noticed their daughter's absence until dinnertime, having assumed she was in her room. By the time the authorities were notified, it was dark and not much could be done until the following morning. Police went door to door asking neighbors if they'd seen or heard anything, and they checked the creek that ran beyond the alley in back of the Elmwood home. The house was searched top to bottom. Miranda's amethyst ring was found in the hallway. Her mother told police that her daughter never took it off.

In the months after the crime, the news reports tapered off. It seemed life went on, but the disappearance was never solved. It was heartbreaking.

There were letters of condolence, curled at the edges and smudged from tears. A gloom settled over the room, as each imagined the pain Miranda's disappearance caused.

In a corner of the chest was a picture of Miranda, sepia-toned, in an oval frame. Under that were several more pictures of Miranda, and of Miranda with her parents. It was odd to see what Miranda looked like when she was alive. They were used to the ethereal girl who had floated into their lives.

Under the scrapbook was a small journal. The handwriting was similar to the note, so they were sure it belonged to Miranda's mother, Elizabeth. Pekin flipped through the book, which was filled with entries, each page crammed with words.

For a moment, she settled in to start reading, but Amber prompted her to see what else was in the cedar chest. "You can read that later. Look how long it is."

"I know, but maybe this is what Miranda wants us to see. Why would she give you the key if there wasn't something important in the trunk?" Pekin said.

"Okay, let's go through the other stuff quickly. Then we can come back to the journal."

Pekin found more old clothes, a box of paper dolls, school textbooks with "Miranda" written on the inside cover, things that were meaningful once upon a time. Amber was disappointed there wasn't a smoking gun.

"It has to be the journal Miranda wants us to see," Pekin said as she returned the ancient items to the trunk.

"I think you're right," Scout said.

"I'll read it tonight," Pekin said. "It shouldn't take long, and I'll take notes of anything that might be important."

The doorbell announced the arrival of the pizza. Scout and Amber hopped up to get plates and napkins from the kitchen as Pekin paid for the pizza.

"What's the plan for tomorrow?" Scout asked, tossing a piece of pepperoni in his mouth.

"We'll talk to Miranda. We need her to give us more details. She knows who her killer is."

"She doesn't want to tell us for some reason."

"But why wouldn't she want us to know?" Amber asked. "Do you think it has to do with the other ghost, the mean one, who keeps telling us to get out?"

"It makes sense. We'll ask her that, too." Pekin picked up the napkins and paper plates. "Scout, can you pick us up again in the morning?"

"Sure."

"I'll meet you guys there," Amber said cryptically. "I need to do something first."

"Like what?" Pekin asked.

"Just something. You'll see tomorrow."

Chapter Twenty-Seven

〰〰〰〰〰〰〰〰〰〰〰〰〰〰〰〰〰〰〰〰〰〰〰

"I DIDN'T FIND ANYTHING in the journal that seemed important," Pekin said, standing in the hallway of Elmwood Manor with Scout.

"Did you read it all the way through?" he asked, a slight frown on his face.

"Yeah. It was really sad when Elizabeth described what went on after her daughter went missing."

"But you didn't find anything that would help us figure out what happened to Miranda?"

"Not really. Elizabeth wrote a lot about searching for her and the devastating blow her disappearance had on the family. How her heart was broken. Stuff like that."

"I think we should read it again. Maybe you missed something due to lack of sleep."

"You're probably right. I might have skimmed through it too quickly. I'll read it again tonight."

They heard a car door and saw Amber coming up the walk.

Scout opened the door to see Amber's smiling face and raised hand holding a small bottle.

"What is it?" Pekin asked.

"Holy Water," she said.

"*What?*"

"Why do you have Holy Water?" Scout asked.

"For protection."

"I think Holy Water is for demons, not ghosts," Pekin said.

"Still. You don't know that for sure. It might come in handy. And, besides, it makes me feel better. Like I have a weapon or something."

"How did you get it?" Scout asked.

Amber frowned. "I might burn in hell for this, but I went to St. Michael's and when the priest wasn't looking I...stole some."

Scout laughed. "I can't believe you did that."

"Well—"

"I'm really proud of you," he said, clapping her on the back.

"I want to do my part," she replied.

"You *are*," Pekin said. "I was so afraid you guys would flake on me. You've both been amazing." She suddenly teared up and turned away so no one would see.

"Aww, Pekie," Amber said, rushing to hug her friend. "Don't worry about me and Scout. We're *in*."

Pekin wiped her eyes. "Sorry, you guys. I don't know why that happened." She pasted on a smile. "I suppose we should try to find Miranda now."

She led the way into the parlor and called out for Miranda. This time, the chill came quickly and Miranda's shimmery form appeared before them.

Miranda seemed somber, not something they'd seen in her before. "Are you okay, Miranda?" Pekin asked.

You shouldn't come here anymore, she said.

"What do you mean? Why not?"

Scout cut in. "Miranda, we need to ask you some things about what happened to you. Can you just talk to us? We won't stay long if you don't want us to."

Miranda looked over her shoulder toward the hallway. She didn't say anything, but nodded and settled onto the sofa in the parlor.

"Don't be scared," Amber said. "We're here to help you."

Scout assumed the role of lead investigator. "We looked through the trunk, but weren't sure what we were looking for. We think it was your mother's cedar chest. There were news reports about your disappearance and some personal items she'd tucked away. And your mother's journal."

Miranda watched him without responding.

"We'll take another look to see if we missed something, but we really need you to tell us everything you can remember of the day you went missing. You said there was a family brunch after church. Was anyone else there besides your immediate family?"

Miranda looked down and smoothed her taffeta skirt with her hands. *My uncle, Edward Moran, the City Councilman. He and his wife were there, and my cousin. And our closest neighbors, the Trents.*

"Who took you, Miranda?" Scout asked, his voice reflecting the urgency they all felt. "Why won't you tell us?"

I can't, she said.

"Why not? What can happen if you tell us?" Amber asked, clearly confused by Miranda's refusal to name her attacker.

Because I'm not alone here, Miranda said, her eyes big. *He won't —.*

"Who else is here with you?" Scout asked.

Just then, the doors upstairs started opening and closing and the air grew heavy and cold.

Get out! a voice boomed from the second floor.

Please, Miranda said. *Go now. Please.*

She shimmered and rushed at Pekin, leaving Pekin shivering as the ghost passed through her. She was too shocked to react, but Scout said, "Let's get out of here," and clutched her arm, pulling her toward the front door.

The three of them grabbed their backpacks and exited the house, whose door slammed shut with no help from them.

"Pekin, what's wrong?" Scout asked in alarm as he noticed that she was shaking. He put his hands on her shoulders and looked into her eyes. "Pekie! Snap out of it." He shook her gently.

She blinked, and threw her arms around his neck. "Oh, Scout. I felt her. She went through me."

He put his arms around her. "You okay?"

After a moment, she nodded.

Pekin pulled back, conscious that she was in Scout's arms; embarrassed but grateful he was so protective.

"What happened?" Amber asked.

"When Miranda left, she came through me. Feel my hands," she said, touching Amber's face. "I'm so cold."

"Her hands are freezing," Amber said to Scout. "It's ninety degrees out here today."

"Let's get her home," he said.

By the time they pulled up to her house, Pekin was back to normal.

Scout put his arm around her shoulders as they walked to the front door. She smiled up at him shyly, very aware of his nearness. "I'm okay. Really."

He seemed reluctant to let her go, but dropped his arm as she pushed open the door.

"You want to read the journal, or do you want me to come in and take a look?" Scout asked.

"I will. And you're right. I was tired last night and may have missed something. I'll read it more carefully tonight."

CHAPTER TWENTY-EIGHT

A FTER HER FRIENDS LEFT, Pekin opened the cedar chest and pulled out the journal. They needed to figure things out quickly. The other ghost was getting more and more aggressive, and Pekin didn't want to fail.

She plopped on her bed and opened the journal. An hour later, she bolted upright, the clue Miranda wanted them to find staring her in the face.

The entries had been difficult to read. Elizabeth's pain at her daughter's disappearance poured out of the pages. More than once, Pekin found herself dabbing at her eyes. And then, there it was. The answer to the mystery of Miranda's disappearance:

No word from the authorities, still. I don't know how I shall survive without my sweet angel. My dear brother Edward and his lovely wife Helen called to offer comfort. They've been so kind to us. It's been hard on Tom, too. He tries to be stoic, but I know he aches as I do. We love our child so deeply. Helen brought a fresh-baked lemon cake. Their thoughtfulness means the world to me. George and Edith Trent came by to invite us to a gallery opening. But poor George. He accidentally chopped off half his finger while clearing brush out of the vacant lot he recently purchased.

Pekin stopped reading. She texted Scout and Amber. *OMG! I found it! I know who killed Miranda.*

She tossed her phone and the journal on her bed and got her

pajamas out of the dresser drawer.

"Griselda, I solved it." She rubbed the little cat's furry head, and kissed its nose. "We can save Miranda now."

She plopped down on the bed and pulled Griselda into a hug, the loud purrs bringing a smile to her face. "I'm so excited."

She stood and put Griselda down on the bed. As she checked the pockets of her hoodie to make sure she hadn't left anything in them, she felt something unexpected and pulled out a familiar black velvet sack. Inside was Miranda's amethyst ring. She stared at it. Had Miranda put it there when she passed through Pekin? She turned it over in her hand, and felt compelled to put it on.

Griselda immediately sat back on her haunches, her little paws dangling in front of her. Her eyes were round and wide, focused on nothing, basically. Pekin cocked her head and watched Griselda as the cat's head turned, its eyes seeming to follow something not visible to Pekin.

Griselda hissed, the hair on her back bristling. Leaping off the bed, her paws hit the floor, and within moments the little cat was nowhere to be seen.

"Whoa," Pekin said softly to the room. "What was that all about?"

That was weird. Pekin closed the door and turned. She nearly jumped out of her skin at the sight of Miranda standing in front of her. Pekin's hand flew to her mouth in surprise.

Don't be afraid, the ghost said.

"But how can you be here?" Pekin asked.

I can go where the ring is. My spirit is attached to it.

"But I thought you couldn't leave the house?"

I couldn't while my ring was there. But now you have it.

"How did you get, you know, stuck in the ring?"

I don't know for sure. My father gave it to me and I always wore it, but when the man was taking me away, I slipped it off my finger hoping it would be found. I wanted someone to know. When he was...was...I focused all my thoughts on the ring to shut out what was happening. So someone would find it and maybe find me.

"But they didn't."

No.

"So…I don't understand. Can you be at both places then?"

I'm not sure. I was at my home until you put on the ring. Now I'm here.

"Is that why you gave it to me?"

Yes.

"Miranda, it was your neighbor, George Trent, wasn't it?"

Miranda was silent.

"I read in your mom's journal that George was missing part of a finger. I figured it had to be him. Was it?"

The ghost nodded. *I thought no one would ever know.*

"Now that we do know, we can help you move on. If that's what you want," Pekin added.

Miranda looked around Pekin's room. Pekin noticed and immediately apologized. "Geez, Miranda. My room's a mess. I didn't know I'd be having company." She stooped and picked up a couple of T-shirts and a pair of flip flops and tossed them in her closet, then snatched a bra off the back of a chair and stuffed it in a drawer. "Sorry."

Miranda laughed. My *mother would have locked me in my room if I let it get messy like this.*

"My mom probably would, too. I don't know. I'm usually very neat. I guess I've been a little preoccupied lately."

Pekin's phone went off and she picked it up. "It's Amber," she said to Miranda before saying hello to Amber.

"Call me back on Facetime," Pekin said, then hit the end call button. When her phone rang again, she could see Amber's face.

"You know who killed Miranda?" was Amber's first question.

"I do. George Trent, the neighbor. And there's something else." She turned the screen of her phone toward the ghost.

"Miranda!" Amber said. "How is she there?"

Pekin held up her hand, wiggling her fingers. "Her ring. She's bound to the ring. She snuck it into my pocket when we were there, so now she's not trapped in Elmwood."

"Can I come over?"

"It's pretty late. You and Scout should come over in the morning. Then we can make some plans."

"Okay," Amber muttered, unable to hide her disappointment.

"Can you call Scout and tell him?"

"Yeah. I'll see you tomorrow," Amber said. "It was great to see you, Miranda."

Pekin put down the phone and sat on her bed. "So, what do we do now? Do you just stick around all night or go back home, or what?"

I'm not sure. I've never done this before. I haven't been out of my house since I...died. But I think if you took off the ring, I wouldn't be here. I will come back when you put it on.

"That makes sense. I mean, as much as any of the rest of this does. I suppose I should say goodnight, though. Big day tomorrow." She started to remove the ring, but paused. "It's just, there are so many things I want to ask you about."

Then ask.

Pekin seemed conflicted. "I would, but I know Scout and Amber will want to hear everything, too, so I should wait for them. I'll let you go for now. See you in the morning."

CHAPTER TWENTY-NINE

P EKIN CLIMBED OUT OF BED and almost hopped into the bathroom to brush her teeth. She was thrilled for what the morning would bring.

She was pulling her hair up into a ponytail when the doorbell rang. She skipped down the stairs and yanked open the front door.

"This is so *exciting*." Amber was practically bouncing as Pekin led Amber and Scout to the den.

Pekin glanced at Scout and smiled. "I couldn't wait until you guys got here."

"Me neither," he replied.

"Call her," Amber said.

Pekin laughed. "Good grief. Do you want to sit down first?" She looked at Scout. "Do you guys want anything before we get started?"

"Water is good," Scout responded. "And chips?"

Pekin rolled her eyes. "Chips? For breakfast? You're so predictable."

She returned moments later with bottles of water under her arm and a big bowl of Doritos. She set everything on the coffee table, then plopped into the chair next to the sofa. Griselda hopped up onto the arm of the chair and promptly curled into a ball, her tail twitching.

Pekin stroked the little cat's head. "Scout, you were right. I reread the journal and the answer was right there."

"What did it say that pointed to Trent?" Scout asked.

"In one of the entries, Miranda's mother mentioned her neighbor dropping by and he was missing half a finger. He had some story about losing it clearing a vacant lot."

"Do we know anything about him?"

"Not so far. I'm hoping that Miranda can fill in some of the details.

Now that she's away from that house." She pulled the black velvet pouch out of her pocket.

As she slipped the ring on her finger, the temperature dropped in the room, followed by a shimmer, and then the ghost was fully present. Griselda let out a yowl and leaped off the chair arm, skidding out of the room.

Scout watched her go. "Weird."

Miranda looked around nervously, before floating to one end of the sofa.

Scout nodded. "Hey."

Miranda smiled shyly and nodded back.

"Do you feel like you can talk more freely being away from your house?" Amber asked.

I think so.

"Was it George Trent?" Scout asked.

Miranda actually looked scared, and the lights in the den flickered.

"Did you make the lights blink like that?" Pekin asked.

When I'm scared or nervous it just happens. I don't mean to.

"We don't mind. We thought that might be what was happening."

"You're safe here," Amber said. "But we need to know, if we're going to help you. Was it George Trent?"

Miranda smoothed her skirt and folded her hands. *Yes.* Her voice was low and timid.

"Why didn't you want to tell us before?" Amber asked.

He wouldn't like it.

"Who wouldn't?" Pekin asked, afraid she already knew the answer.

Mr. Trent.

"Wait. He's at Elmwood with you?" Amber asked.

She nodded.

"How do you live there with him?" Scout asked. "I can't even imagine—"

I can't leave. I stay as quiet as I can, and I try to hide from him.

"Can he find you?"

If he wants to. Sometimes he gets tired of searching and leaves me alone.

"Where is he? We haven't seen him," Pekin said.

There's a place he goes. He's content to stay there. But sometimes he looks for me.

No one said anything.

"What does he do then?" Pekin asked, holding her breath.

He takes me back. He makes me relive that moment over and over. It's the only pleasure he gets.

"That moment? Oh my goodness, Miranda. That's awful. I'm so sorry," Amber proclaimed. "Can he do anything else? Could he hurt us?"

I don't know, Miranda said. *He only cares about me.*

"*Cares* about you?" Pekin stared at her in disbelief.

He believes he owns me. He gets pleasure from tormenting me, scaring me. Hurting me. But he knows about you now. He listens.

Pekin shivered as a chill ran up her spine. Looking at Amber, Pekin knew she wasn't alone.

"We have to get you away from him. If you can leave the house, can you move on now?" Pekin asked.

No. The ring binds me.

"What do we have to do to unbind you?" Pekin asked.

I believe, if you find my...bones. Maybe then.

"Do you know where they are?" Scout asked.

Miranda twisted her hands in her lap and shook her head. *It's dark.*

"But—"

I have no knowledge of their location.

"That makes it a little more challenging," Pekin said.

"What do you remember?" Amber asked.

I couldn't see because it was dark. I smelled dankness, dampness. Dirt.

"Nothing else?"

No. I...wait. There were leaves. In a sack.

"Leaves in a sack." Scout seemed to consider it. "Could it have been the garden shed?"

Miranda was silent for a moment. *Yes, maybe.*

Pekin met Scout's eyes. "It happened in the garden shed. Do you think he might have left her there?"

"She would have been found," Scout said. "Unless—"

"Unless he covered her up with something or buried her," Amber said. "We have to go find out if she's there."

"You down with that, Miranda?" Scout asked.

She looked at him questioningly.

"I mean, are you okay with us searching the shed?"

I'm afraid, she said.

"Until we are able to find your...your—" Scout stammered.

"Resting place," Pekin said helpfully.

"Right. Until we can locate your resting place, we can't save you. We have to find where he left you, so you'll be free to move on."

"It's settled then," Pekin said. "Let's go save Miranda."

MIRANDA WAS ENTHRALLED with the experience of riding in a car. It was so unlike anything she would have experienced in her short lifetime. Her head almost swiveled on her neck as she tried to look everywhere at once, taking in the ways the city had changed since her passing.

"It's cool that you can hang out with us this way," Amber said. "If we had more time, we could drive you around Springdale so you could see what the city looks like now."

Miranda smiled, her face still reflecting wonder at how different everything was a century after her death.

"Do you have any suggestions for dealing with George Trent, Miranda?" Scout asked.

She seemed to shrink. *I don't know*, she whispered. Then she sat up straighter and said, *I don't know what he can do. His will is stronger than mine*. She looked down at her hands, which were clenched in her lap. *I'm sorry.*

No one spoke for a moment, then Scout said, "Maybe we should let Miranda stay in the car when we go in."

Pekin looked at him.

"She's afraid, and what we do might make him try to stop us. She can't fight him, I'm not sure we can either, but maybe she should be somewhere he can't reach her."

"Miranda?" Pekin asked.

The ghost looked too afraid to speak.

"Do you want to stay here in the car instead of going inside?" Pekin asked.

When Miranda looked up, the fear in her eyes was all the answer any of them needed. As they pulled up in front of Elmwood, Pekin removed the ring from her finger and dropped it into the black velvet pouch. The ghost vanished. "I'll leave it in the glove compartment until we're done," Pekin said.

No one was in a hurry to get out of the car. Despite the sun peeking among the clouds, it felt like a blanket of evil covered Elmwood. For the first time, Pekin was reluctant to step inside.

Chapter Thirty

~~~~~~

PEKIN TOOK THE KEY from her pocket as they walked up to the porch.

"Wait," Amber said. "I know you guys think it was a stupid idea, but I put the Holy Water in spray bottles for us. I think we should all have them."

"Nothing's a stupid idea. Not given what we're up against," Pekin said as she took the small bottle from Amber. "Thanks. I feel safer already."

She held her breath and pushed open the front door. The house felt empty. No one wanted to speak for fear of alerting George Trent's ghost to their presence.

"We should get the shed key and go out back," Scout said, breaking the silence.

Amber pointed out the window. "We picked a great day for this. It's started sprinkling. Just what we need, rain."

It was because the summer storm had turned the sky dark that Amber could see their reflections in the front room window. She started toward Pekin and Scout when she saw another figure in the reflection. She let out a shriek and whirled toward the foyer. Scout and Pekin both turned to see what was upsetting her as a voice boomed out, ***WHERE IS SHE?***

The large translucent image of a man stood in the doorway, his face scrunched into a terrifying grimace of rage. ***WHERE IS MIRANDA?***

Scout stepped forward and said, "She's not here anymore."

Don't try me, boy, the ghost demanded.

"George Trent." Pekin stepped up to stand beside Scout. "You killed Miranda. You're a *murderer*."

As he surged forward in a threatening manner, Amber, Holy

Water in hand, sprayed the ghost. Following her lead, Scout and Pekin lifted their spray bottles and also sprayed.

Howls from the entity filled the room, which turned bitterly cold as an icy wind swirled from out of nowhere, carrying loose items up in its vortex. An angry aura of energy flashed around the ghost as he yelled and swung out his arms. Vases and lamps crashed to the floor, paintings flew from the walls. The kids ducked and covered their heads to protect themselves from the flying objects. Pekin screamed when the ghost picked her up and yanked her toward the door. Scout ran toward her, but the ghost flipped his hand and Scout was flung backward and lay crumpled at the foot of a heavy side table. Amber yelled as the ghost dragged Pekin out of the room, moving so quickly all Amber saw was the blur of their passing. The door slammed, with Amber and Scout still inside. Amber ran to the door but couldn't get it open. She frantically pulled on the knob, then looked over her shoulder at Scout, torn over which of her friends to help. Scout had the most obvious need as he lay bleeding on the floor, and she ran to his side to help him sit up.

George Trent's voice filled the room. ***You want to know what happened to Miranda? I'll show you exactly what happened to Miranda.*** Ghostly laughter permeated the house.

Scout tried to sit up and shook his head to clear it. Blood trickled from a gash on his forehead where his head hit a corner of the table. Amber offered a hand and pulled him shakily to his feet.

"Where did they go?" he asked, swaying as he lifted a hand to his head.

"I don't know. He slammed the door so I couldn't see where they went."

The door still refused to open, but after a few tugs by Scout it gave way. Scout and Amber stood in the hallway looking for a clue as to which way the ghost and Pekin had gone, to no avail. They headed toward the back of the house, but when they got to the end of the hall nothing was there. They looked at each other in bewilderment.

Pekin's voice floated weakly to them on the frigid breeze that had spun around the ghost as it fled with her. It seemed to come from the walls themselves. "Help me!" she called out, before her plea was cut short.

Amber shouted her name, but there was no response. She grabbed Scout's arm. "Where could they have gone?" Her eyes were big as saucers. She swiped at the tears streaming down her face.

Scout pounded the wall in frustration, then ducked into the kitchen and mudroom, calling her name. There was no sign of her, and no sense of a presence. Nothing but silence. He turned and ran toward the stairs, Amber close on his heels. Neither the second floor nor the attic gave any clues to the location of their friend, so they rushed back downstairs and checked the library and dining room. Another empty search.

"Let her go!" Amber screamed as Scout looked out the backdoor toward the shed. The door of the shed was closed and the key hung on the hook by the mudroom door.

"We need help," Amber cried out. She raced back to the foyer to rummage through her backpack for the business card she'd saved. Just in case. She pulled her phone from her jeans pocket and punched in the number.

After several rings, "Hello" echoed from the other end.

Amber's voice shook as she spoke. "Hello? Mrs. Willingham? We need you."

By the time Mildew arrived, Scout and Amber had given up their fruitless search and were sitting dejectedly on the bottom step of the stairs.

Amber opened the door as soon as Mildew knocked. "Okay, fill me in," the small woman said breathlessly, noting the expressions of shock and grief she saw on the faces before her.

"The ghost took Pekin," Amber said. "We don't know where they went. He was a murderer. He killed Miranda and now he has Pekin."

"What happened, exactly?"

Scout and Amber both talked at once, and Mildew had to tell them to slow down. Scout glanced at Amber and then said, "We have an idea of where Miranda's body might be."

Mildew held up her hand. "First, back up a bit. Who is Miranda?"

"She lived in this house. She was murdered in 1918 and her ghost lives here. Or maybe not *lives* here, but you know what I mean,"

Amber said.

"She haunts this house. I understand."

"Miranda's ghost needs us to find her remains, so she can be properly buried and move on," Scout said. "Her body was never found. And she wouldn't tell us who killed her, and then we found out that it was her neighbor and his ghost is here, too. And she's afraid of him."

"She bit off his finger," Amber added helpfully.

"Ewww." Mildew scrunched up her face.

"That's what I said, too," Amber responded.

Mildew held up her hand, closing her eyes and breathing quietly for a moment.

"I feel a presence here, but just one. I thought there were two ghosts?"

"Miranda's out in the car," Amber said.

"How can she be?" Mildew asked. "Isn't she bound to this house?"

"That's what we thought, too," Scout said, "but she's actually bound to a ring. Long story but Miranda slipped the ring into Pekin's pocket. When Pekin discovered it later at home and tried it on, Miranda appeared in Pekin's bedroom. Miranda's afraid of the other ghost so we thought she'd be safer in the car, and that's where we left the ring."

"Hmm," Mildew said, considering. "So, tell me, where are Miranda's remains to be found?"

"We think in the garden shed in the backyard. Miranda remembered smells of dirt and leaves. Anyway, we left her in the car so that we could go search the shed."

"But the other ghost could tell she was gone so he came screaming in yelling at us to tell him where she was. Then we sprayed him with Holy Water," Amber said breathlessly.

"Holy Water?" Mildew asked.

"I thought it couldn't hurt. That's what exorcists use. It made him really mad. That's when he started throwing things around and took Pekin."

"I can imagine the ghost hated it."

"But he has *Pekin*," Amber said. "What do we do?"

Mildew sighed. "We can start searching room by room. The ghost can't leave here, so that means they're in this house."

"Or the shed," Scout added.

"I'm not sure why the killer's ghost haunts this house." Mildew narrowed her eyes in thought.

"We think it's because of the finger," Scout said.

"She swallowed it," Amber added.

"Ewww," Mildew said.

"I know," Amber replied.

"Yes, that could explain it."

"How could they vanish like that?" Scout asked. "I know George Trent could vanish, but what about Pekin?"

"That we must find out."

"Let's start searching then," Scout said.

"You know what to look for, right?" Mildew asked. "Cold spots, maybe you feel a presence, things like that?"

"Yes. We've felt the temperature drop when Miranda came into the room. And then today when George did. His presence was way colder than Miranda's."

"I believe that's the evil in him. He, perhaps, has been working on enhancing his abilities over these many years. Let's check every room down here and then we can go upstairs."

"We checked all the rooms," Scout said. "We didn't see which way they went."

"What can he do to Pekin?" Amber asked.

Mildew looked troubled. "Let's not worry about that now. We should look for your friend."

"We didn't find any sign of them," Scout said. "Can the ghost make her invisible?"

"No. There's a physical angle we have to discover. She's human so she can't pass through walls like a ghost can. Which means there's a hiding place somewhere in this house. Let's go take a look." Small and round though she was, Mildew moved quickly and determinedly down the hall.

Chapter Thirty-One

"**I** THINK WE NEED THE EMF," Mildew said.

"What's an EMF?" Amber asked.

"It's an electromagnetic field detector. It reads energy. A strong reading could indicate the presence of a ghost. I have one in my car. I always have tools of the trade with me, just in case."

"Hello?" Pekin's mom, Melissa, stuck her head in the open front door. "She took a few steps inside the hallway. "Anyone here?"

Scout and Amber came out of the kitchen, followed by a small round woman that Melissa didn't know.

"Where's Pekin? I thought you kids could use lunch, so I brought—" Melissa noticed the stricken faces. "What's wrong? Where's Pekin?"

"Mrs. Dewlap," Scout began, then stopped.

The small woman stepped around him and said, "Mrs. Dewlap? I'm Mildred Willingham. The kids called me because your daughter has...uh...she's missing."

"*What?* Where's my daughter?" Melissa's face turned pale.

"I'm afraid this house is haunted."

"I know all about Miranda," Melissa said. "I met her."

"Besides Miranda, there's another entity in residence. This entity was angry because Miranda isn't in the house, and he's taken Pekin."

Melissa pulled her cell out of her back pocket and started to punch in numbers. "I'm calling the police."

Before the phone could ring, Mildew put her hand on Melissa's arm. "That won't do any good. I will find your daughter. The police will think we're all crazy. Please hang up."

Before the 911 operator answered, Melissa hit the "End" button. "*I* think you're all crazy. The idea of poking around in a haunted house, of imagining yourselves as cold case detectives.... How could you let them do this?" she directed at Mildew.

"I assure you, I had no idea what was going on here. In fact, I offered my services to the young people weeks ago, but they seemed to believe they were quite capable of—"

"They're children! They only *think* they're capable of... of...*anything*. What is a ghost going to do with my daughter?"

Mildew again placed a calming hand on Melissa's arm. "That's what we're in the process of finding out. I've had experience with these entities before. If you will allow me—"

"Allow you to what? What can you do?"

"As I was explaining to the children before your arrival, I have tools in my car. I should be able to track the energy put off by the ghost. When we locate him, we'll locate your daughter."

"Well, hurry. *Hurry!*" Melissa's face, which was already pale, grew stark, all expression gone.

Mildew headed to her car, trailed by Scout and Amber. She handed the EMF reader to Scout and boxes of salt and sage bundles to Amber, then slammed the trunk lid and hurried back up the walk. She immediately approached Melissa, begging for time to work her magic.

"We're going to go room to room with the EMF reader. It will at least give us an idea of where they might be." She switched on the meter and held it in front of her as she walked into the parlor. "There's energy here."

"Of course. That's where George Trent grabbed Pekin," Amber said.

Mildew returned to the hall and walked toward the back of the house. There were bursts of static and the needle on the EMF dial jumped around. "Energy here, as well." She entered the kitchen, holding the EMF reader up, shaking it slightly when it didn't react. "Hmm. No energy in this room, so they didn't come this way."

She headed back to the hallway, trailed by Amber, Scout, and Melissa. Mildew held the reader in front of her as she entered the mudroom. "The energy doesn't appear in this room."

"You mean it just stops?" Melissa asked, her voice rising with panic.

"Yes. The energy seems to have moved on from here. We'll try upstairs." She headed for the stairs.

Melissa stepped into the parlor and called her husband. "Edward, Pekin is missing." Pekin's father didn't immediately register the direness of the situation. "I'm sure she's just with her friends. Nothing to worry about."

"No! You don't *understand*. She's at that *house*. The one she and her friends are obsessed with. Can you come here?"

"Well, I—"

"Edward, I need you. What if they can't find her?"

"Now, Mellie, it will be okay. I'll leave now. What's the address?"

"Hurry, Edward. I'm scared."

"Did you call the police?"

Melissa hesitated. "No, I…I started to but—"

She stopped, not sure what to say. "When I got here, Scout and Amber were here, and a woman who is helping them search. The woman said it wouldn't do any good to call the police."

"And why wouldn't it do any good?"

"Well, she said…she said that an *entity* took Pekin and that the police wouldn't understand."

"*I* don't understand. Don't worry. I'm on my way."

In the half hour it took for Edward Dewlap to get there, the police were already at the front door. Since the door stood open, they announced their presence, and entered the hallway. Melissa, who'd been upstairs with the searchers, rushed down the stairs to greet them when she heard them call out, followed closely by Scout and Amber.

"We had a call about a missing teenage girl?" one of the officers asked.

"Yes. It's my daughter, Pekin. My husband called you?"

"Yes, ma'am. I'm Officer Carter, and this is my partner, Officer Elliott. What can you tell us about your daughter's disappearance?"

"Her friends were with her when it happened. They can tell you more than I can."

Scout and Amber looked at each other. These cops weren't going to buy the ghost story.

Officer Elliott flipped open his notebook and looked expectantly at Scout. "Did you see what happened?" he asked.

"Um, yes. We were all together in the parlor there."

Before Scout could continue, Edward arrived like a whirlwind barking out questions.

"The kids were just about to tell us what happened," Officer Carter said.

Edward glared at Scout. "Where's Pekin? What happened?"

Chapter Thirty-Two

PEKIN HUDDLED IN A CORNER of the dark cement room, screaming.

No one can hear you, the ghost of George Trent growled. *They won't find you either*, he added with a creepy grin. *Very thick.* He knocked on the wall behind him. *See? It's solid.*

"Let me go!" she squeaked. The large wavery form glared down at her. Pekin covered her face with her hands and said, "Please. I don't want to be here."

It was cold and damp, and she shivered. But not from the cold. Her teeth chattered in fear of what was to come.

Gradually, as her eyes adjusted to the darkness, she could make out a large room, empty except for a chair and a folding table. She noticed a door to her right and scrambled to her feet. Before she could launch herself at the door, the ghost towered over her, reaching out his hands and tracing them along her face and down her arms, causing her to gasp at the icy touch of his fingers.

It's time for me to have a new playmate.

Pekin cried out in pain as he wrapped his fingers around her head. She felt them squeezing through her skull, into her brain. *Wait 'til I show you everything.* This time, the voice was coming from inside her. She panted in fear. She felt her head filling as if it would explode from the pressure. A hollow evil laugh caused her body to shake. *Pay attention now*, the voice said.

As visions began to play out behind her eyes, she slumped to the floor, no longer aware of the dampness of the cold cement.

SCOUT TRIED TO LOOK MORE ADULT than he felt. "I'm sure you're going to find this very hard to believe." He glanced at Amber, who tried to look as encouraging as she could muster.

"Get to it. Where's my daughter?" Edward had gone to anger as soon as he arrived.

"Give him a chance, dear," Melissa said, putting a hand on his arm.

Edward started to shake it off, then seemed to get himself under control. "All right. Can you please tell me where my daughter is?"

"George Trent took her."

"Who's George Trent?" Edward asked.

"Mr. Dewlap, please let us do our job," Officer Carter said. "We need to be methodical to make sure we get all the information possible as soon as possible."

"Okay, but—"

"What can you tell us about George Trent?" the officer asked Scout.

"He's a ghost, sir," Scout said sheepishly.

"My daughter is *missing*. Stop that silliness," Edward said, the anger on his face threatening.

"Edward," Melissa said pleadingly. "Please. Just listen. Let him tell us what happened."

"Go on, young man," Officer Elliott said. "You said George Trent. Who is that exactly?"

"I'm trying to tell you. I know it sounds crazy, but it's what happened. Sir, this house is haunted."

In the background, Edward sputtered and only Officer Elliott holding up a warning hand caused him to remain silent.

"Haunted?" Officer Elliott was writing methodically in his notebook. "In what way?"

"Well, Pekin and I, and Amber, we have this company Pekin started to rid haunted houses of ghosts. This is our first job. The first ghost we met—"

"The *first* ghost?" Officer Elliott asked.

"Yes, sir. That was Miranda. Miranda Talbert. She was murdered in 1918 and her ghost is trapped here. We were trying to help her cross over."

"Officer, you can't seriously be considering this ridiculous story. Ask him what really happened." Edward looked ready to beat a confession out of Scout.

"Mr. Dewlap," Amber said. "Scout's telling the truth. I was here, too. We both saw George Trent's ghost grab Pekin and drag her down the hall. Look at the bump on Scout's head. The ghost threw him against a wall. Then we couldn't find where they went." She looked at Melissa for help. "Mrs. Dewlap, you know about Miranda. Tell them."

"Let me," a voice said, and Mildew descended the stairs to join them in the hallway.

"And who are you?" Officer Elliott asked.

"My name is Mildred Willingham. The children called me when their friend went missing and I rushed over to help get her back."

"What's your relationship to the missing girl?"

"I've only met her once. I offered my help with this house. Amber called me in a panic and I rushed over. We were in the process of trying to find her when you all arrived."

"Why is your name familiar?" Officer Carter asked.

"Probably because I've worked with Captain Burroughs in the past. Perhaps you know of me from him?"

"You're the ghost lady, right?"

"I suppose that's a correct description. Captain Burroughs will vouch for me if need be."

"Okay, Ms. Willingham, what can you tell us about what happened here?"

"Scout and Amber are telling you the truth. There is another entity in this house. An evil one. It was responsible for the murder of Miranda Talbert and has been trapped here with her for more than a century. The children have been working to release Miranda's spirit to move on, and when George Trent found out, he wanted revenge. George Trent's ghost took Pekin."

The officers and Edward stared open-mouthed at Mildew. Edward grunted in frustration. "You aren't buying this, are you?" He confronted both officers.

"Please, Mr. Dewlap. Let us take care of this."

"We don't have time to stand around gabbing. Why aren't you

looking for my daughter?"

"Let us just get everyone's statements, then we'll know how to proceed."

"You proceed by looking for my daughter!" Edward snapped.

Officer Elliott wiped his hand over his face in an effort to maintain his composure. "I understand your frustration, Mr. Dewlap. We'll definitely look for your daughter. Now, if you'll let us continue with our interviews...."

He turned to Mildew. "You realize how preposterous that sounds, do you not?"

"Of course. My whole life, I've been aware of how people perceive what I tell them. That doesn't make it any less real. Scout is telling you the truth, and I'm your best chance of finding Pekin Dewlap."

Another cop cruiser had pulled up out front and two more officers were heading up the walkway. Officer Carter stepped outside and the three of them conferred in lowered voices. When they entered the foyer, Officer Carter introduced Officers Martin and Sanchez, then directed them to begin searching the house, one heading upstairs and one covering the main floor.

As Mildew and the two teens didn't budge on their version of the facts, Officer Elliott excused them, trying to clear the crime scene. None of them wanted to leave, however, and retreated only as far as the front yard where they could still hear how the investigation was proceeding.

As the officers spoke with Melissa and Edward, doors on the second floor started slamming one after another and a booming voice said **Get out!**

Scout, Amber and Mildew ran back inside. "Now do you believe us?" Scout asked urgently.

Two of the officers rushed upstairs, as Officer Martin insisted he had checked every room and he was sure no one was on the second floor.

Officer Elliott brushed off Scout's question, calling out to ask if the officers found anything upstairs. After five minutes, the two policemen came back to the foyer with nothing to report.

"I want everyone out of here," Officer Elliott said amid protests.

"We need to secure the crime scene."

"You need to let us get her back, Officer," said Scout. "You won't be able to deal with George Trent."

"Let us worry about that. In the meantime, out."

Once outside again, Edward turned on the three ghost hunters. "I think you're lying. If you hurt my daughter, you'll live to regret it."

"Mr. Dewlap, it wasn't us. It was George——"

"There is no George Trent. You're hiding something."

Melissa tried to calm her husband down. "Edward, they might be right."

He whirled on her. "You're taking their side?"

"I'm not taking anybody's side. It's just…there really is a ghost. At least one. I've seen her."

"What do you mean you've seen a ghost? And you said it's a she."

"The ghost I met…yes, I met her and I spoke with her…anyway, the ghost I met was Miranda Talbert. The kids have been working to try to help her cross over. You know about Pekin's business. You said you were okay with it."

"I didn't take it seriously. I thought it was a whim."

"What do you think Pekin's been working so diligently on every day for weeks? She's been here at Elmwood, with Scout and Amber, trying to find out what's holding Miranda here. And they figured it out. The kids figured out what happened to Miranda in 1918."

"Don't be ridiculous," Edward blustered.

"Edward, do you really think I would lie to you? We've been married more than twenty years. In all that time you haven't learned to trust me?"

Edward was silent for a moment. "Of course, I don't think you'd lie, especially about something so important. But you——"

"But nothing. I haven't lost my mind. I actually saw a ghost, a real live ghost that you could see right through." She looked at her husband pleadingly, placing a hand on his arm. "They found an old trunk in the attic of this house and went through everything in it looking for clues. Pekin discovered an entry in an old journal that pointed to their neighbor as the man who took Miranda. That man's ghost is the one that took Pekin. I believe the kids."

He sighed. "So, what do we do now?"

Mildew stepped up. "Mr. Dewlap, I know you're having trouble accepting this, but I can assure you that it is possible, in fact it's likely, that a ghost took your daughter. The police won't be able to help you. You must let us go find Pekin."

"And who are you, exactly?" Edward asked.

"I'm Mildred Willingham. I've been able to see spirits since I was a little girl. All of my adult life it's been my mission to help ghosts move on from this plane. I know how to deal with them. George Trent has your daughter somewhere in the house. His spirit is bound to this house so he can't leave it. We've already searched both floors using my EMF meter."

At Edward's confused look, Mildew continued. "It's a device that basically measures energy spikes. Ghosts often cause energy spikes that can be read by the EMF. However, since it didn't provide us with any clues, we need to think about what he could have done with Pekin."

"We're not leaving here without our daughter," Edward said.

"We're not leaving either," Mildew replied. "Until the police let us back inside, we should try to figure this out."

"Mildew," Amber said timidly. "Can we ask Miranda if there are any hiding places we might not know about?"

"That's brilliant, Amber," Mildew responded. "Do you know how we can talk to her?"

"Pekin left the ring in Scout's car. I think if I put on the ring she'll appear."

"She's right," Scout said. "It's definitely worth a try." He pulled his car key out of his pocket and unlocked the passenger side door. In a moment he was back with the black velvet bag and handed it to Amber.

"We shouldn't call her back here, though, should we?" Amber asked. "What if George can sense her and goes after her, too?"

"Hmm," Mildew said. "I think it would be prudent if we found another location. Your car, maybe?" she addressed Scout.

"My car's pretty small for all of us," he said, "but we can try—"

"What about the park?" Melissa said. "It's a block away. It should be safe for her there. I can drive." She looked at her husband. "You're going to want to see this."

CHAPTER THIRTY-THREE

THE SMALL GROUP piled into Melissa's SUV. From his demeanor, it was obvious Edward knew he was just along for the ride. Others were running the show. Moments after pulling into the park, they were gathered around a picnic table in a corner of the park that was mostly empty of visitors, looking expectantly at Amber.

She held her breath and slid the ring on her finger. Nothing happened. "It's not working," Amber cried, disappointment evident in her eyes.

"Are there too many of us?" Scout asked.

"But we all want to hear this," Amber said.

"Talk to her for a minute. Tell her who we all are and that we really need her help. She may be reluctant to appear with strangers present," Mildew said.

"Okay, I'll try again." Amber looked hard at the ring and turned it on her finger several times, then closed her eyes. "Miranda, something's happened. Pekin needs you. You're the only one who can help us...help her. George Trent took her. We were going to try to find your bones and while we were in the house George got mad because you were gone. He grabbed Pekin and ran off with her. We've looked everywhere. All through the house. But we couldn't find any sign of her. Mildew...This is Mildew. She came to help us. She took her EMF meter through the house but it didn't turn up anything. And Pekin's mom and dad are here, too. Everyone's worried about her. Miranda, we don't know where else to look. Are there any hiding places in your house where he could have taken her?"

All eyes were on Amber, waiting to see what would happen. After a pause, the air shimmered and Miranda materialized at the end of the picnic table. Edward gasped. "That's...that's a *ghost*," he said pointing.

"Told you," Melissa whispered.

Miranda looked timidly at the assembled group and then said, *I'm sorry Pekin has vanished. I believe I know where he would take her. Because he took me there. A hidden passage leads to a stairway going down into an old storage room. The passage was boarded over and repainted during a modernization of the kitchen. The architect left a trigger that opens the passageway. It's off the back hallway just before the backdoor.*

"How do we find it?" Scout asked.

As you go toward the mudroom, if you look closely at the wainscoting on the left wall you will see a small, almost unnoticeable button within it. The doorway is camouflaged by the panels on the wall. If you push the button, the wall will swing open. That is most surely where he would go. She looked down.

"What could he do to my daughter?" Edward asked.

Miranda didn't answer immediately. *He can scare her. To death.*

"*What?*" Melissa cried in alarm. "What do you mean?"

He can go into her thoughts and show her terrible things. He can make her think he can do those terrible things to her. It's best if you find her quickly. That's all I can say.

And then she was gone. Amber took the ring off and dropped it into the velvet bag, then handed it to Melissa. "To hold for Pekin. She'll want it back."

Mildew stood. "We need to get in that house. Somehow, we have to convince the police to let us find that hidden storage place."

"Do you think Miranda would tell the police herself?" Amber asked.

"I really doubt it. She was uneasy with our group and she knows two of you already. We can always try if that's our only option. But, first, let's go back and try to talk our way in."

Mildew looked shrewdly at Amber. "I hate to ask this, but are you willing to stage another robbery at St. Michael's?"

"What are you talking about?" Melissa asked.

"Holy Water. We could use some Holy Water."

"How do we get Holy Water? Do we ask the Father?" Melissa looked confused.

"No. Not when we have our very own cat burglar," Scout said.

"Amber?"

"Really?" Amber brightened, pleased that Mildew valued her contribution. "Sure. Mrs. Dewlap, can you swing by St. Michael's on the way back?"

"We don't have time for this!" Edward spluttered. "Every minute we waste—"

"I assure you, Mr. Dewlap, this isn't a waste of time. The more weapons we have at our disposal when we confront George Trent, the better our chances."

Edward scowled. "Okay, fine. But can we hurry it up?"

To give Amber cover, Melissa and Edward went into the church with her. As Amber dug a water bottle out of her backpack and emptied it in the bushes beside the walkway, Father Carlo appeared to welcome them and offer his assistance. Melissa looked at Edward and said "Do you have a minute, Father? Our daughter is missing and words of comfort from you could bring us hope that we find her safe."

"Of course, would you like to step into my study?"

"Yes, please," Melissa said. "Edward?"

The two of them followed behind Father Carlo. The moment the three of them were out of sight, Amber dipped the water bottle in the Holy Water receptacle and peered around nervously as it slowly filled. Sweat prickled her forehead as she whispered "*hurry, hurry*" under her breath. Once she was satisfied, she put the cap on the bottle and tried to look innocent as she waited for the Dewlaps to return.

It was a short wait. The priest followed Melissa and Edward back to the front of the church, saying, "I wish you didn't have to leave so soon. I don't feel I've offered you adequate comfort in your time of need."

"You were great, Father," Melissa said, taking his hand and giving it a gentle squeeze. "But we need to get back to our search. Thank you for taking the time to speak to us." She took Edward's arm and nodded at Amber, and the three of them hurried from the church.

"Did you get it?" Mildew asked as soon as the car doors were closed.

Amber held up the nearly full bottle. "Is this enough?"

"Yes. We don't need to drown him, just spray a little on him. It's very powerful stuff."

The police weren't happy to see them back at the front door, but Edward took the lead and insisted that he be allowed to do his own search. "She's *my* daughter," he protested when Officer Elliott resisted the suggestion. It seemed a standoff, until the officer agreed to back off for an hour and give the Dewlaps and the ghost hunters the run of the house. Mildew's threat to call her friend the Captain may have buttered the rails a bit.

Mildew held her ghost supplies and Amber's Holy Water as they headed toward the back of the house. Scout raced ahead and searched the wainscoting. "It's here!"

Each of them carried a spray bottle newly filled with the Holy Water. Amber clutched hers tightly, apprehension building as a portion of the wall suddenly swung inward, a waft of stale air assaulting them.

It was dark and musty in the passageway. Scout handed one of the flashlights he'd brought with him to Edward. He shined the beam ahead of him in the cramped corridor and highlighted the stairs leading down to a closed door.

"We should be as quiet as we can," Mildew whispered. "If we can surprise him, it might work in our favor."

Scout and Mildew descended the stairs first, and Scout took hold of the doorknob. He looked at Mildew and she nodded. He turned the knob and pushed the door open.

"Is she there?" Edward whispered frantically before Melissa shushed him.

Pekin lay curled in a fetal position on the stone floor. Scout rushed toward her when a blast of frigid air flung him back into Edward and the others following behind.

They clambered to their feet and tumbled into the room as George Trent materialized. ***She's mine. Get out!***

The spirit waved his hand and spiders fell from the ceiling onto the unsuspecting rescuers. All but Mildew shrieked and brushed frantically at their hair and clothes.

"They're not real," Mildew said, her voice authoritative. "He's causing you to imagine them. Ignore the spiders and they'll go away."

Too over the edge to listen, Amber still squealed in fright. Mildew said sternly, "They're not *real*. Stop reacting and they'll vanish."

Amber didn't appear to be reassured, but she stopped moving, hunching her shoulders and squeezing her eyes shut, and immediately the spiders were gone. She tentatively opened one eye, then straightened up when she saw it was all clear.

George Trent lunged at Mildew. She raised her spray bottle and unleashed a torrent of Holy Water in his face. He screamed out in rage, then, laughing maniacally, he turned and dove into the still figure of Pekin.

"Oh, no!" Mildew moaned.

"What just happened?" Melissa asked. "Where did he go?"

All eyes turned toward Pekin who was pushing herself up from the floor. Slowly at first, and then she shot to her feet. Her eyes were wild and angry.

"Grab her," Mildew shouted. "That's not Pekin. George Trent has invaded her. We must restrain her. Scout, quick, get a hold on her before she can harm herself or anyone else."

He looked at her in confusion.

"Scout! *Hurry!*"

A growl came from Pekin and she advanced toward them. Scout jumped behind her and threw his arms around her, which caused her to scream in rage. She twisted easily out of his arms with seemingly superhuman strength.

Edward, who'd watched in shock, leaped forward and grappled with her as Scout again attempted to pin her arms to her sides. "Rope!" Mildew screamed. "In my car. We need the rope."

Melissa sprinted up the stairs and out into the hallway. As she burst out the front door, Officer Elliott attempted to intercept her but she yelled at him to get out of her way. Over her shoulder she called, "Go help them," and pointed toward the backdoor.

Officer Elliott gestured for Officer Carter as he hurried down the hallway. By the time they arrived in the small storage room, Melissa arrived with the rope.

"Officers, please. We have to secure her before she can hurt someone."

Chapter Thirty-Four

THE PRESSURE BUILT IN PEKIN'S HEAD, like cotton was filling up the space and shoving her into a tight corner where she was too cramped to move. She was helpless as her body squirmed and lashed out. Her throat vibrated with the growls and snarls emanating from her mouth. She felt the urge to scratch eyes and strangle anyone close enough to reach. Pekin didn't want to feel that way, but she was powerless against the force in control of her body and mind. She moaned softly, a sound no one outside of her head could hear.

Scout was nearest to her. She strained against the force that urgently desired to hurt him, frustrated at her weakness in the face of whatever was in control of her body. Not Scout! She adored him. He was *her* Scout. Pekin felt the hatred and rage pouring out toward him. She dug deep into her psyche and tried to force her hands into the giant cotton ball that was threatening to shove her all the way out of her head. Her fingers penetrated the cotton ball, which turned out to be sticky and snotty. Ewww! Even as she groped around in the foreign entity in her head, the cotton ball's slimy interior oozed around her fingers, hardening into a grip that tried to trap them. She snatched her hands back in horror. All of this was a horror, and she couldn't do anything to help herself. She tried to scream out, "I'm still in here! I'm here! Don't leave me behind!" but no one heard her small voice over the inhuman sounds coming from the mouth controlled by the cotton ball.

INSTEAD OF ASSISTING THEM, Officer Elliott immediately questioned the treatment the newly discovered victim was receiving and ordered that Pekin be released, but Mildew stood up to him. "We cannot...I repeat, *cannot*...release this girl. She has been invaded by a ghost. George

Trent was a murderer and now he's trying to control a new body that will let him continue his misdeeds. Look at her. Listen to her. Does that sound normal to you?"

"She needs a hospital, not to be treated like this. Get that rope off her before I take all of you in."

"Officer, you didn't see her when we found her. You weren't here when the ghost took over my daughter. You need to let us get her back," Edward said.

"This is ridiculous," Officer Elliott sputtered.

"Officer Elliott," Mildew said. "Call Detective Burroughs if you don't believe me. He'll back me up, I assure you. You have to get out of our way."

"I don't *have* to do anything. I want you out of this room. Now."

He approached Pekin, who whipped her head toward him. He put a hand on her arm and said, "You're going to be okay now."

Without warning, Pekin's head darted forward, her teeth sinking into his shoulder. He let out a scream and jerked back in pain. When he reached up to touch the injured shoulder, his hand came away bloody. He took a step back in shock. Officer Carter rushed forward to help him, shouting into his radio "Officer down," and rushing Officer Elliott out of the room and up the stairs.

Mildew immediately slammed the door and flipped the latch, locking the police outside. "Quick. Make sure the ropes are secure."

Scout tugged on the rope coils, ensuring they were tight enough. Then, he and Edward gently propped the squirming girl so that she was sitting against a wall.

Scout sank onto the floor against the opposite wall where Amber joined him. He rubbed his face, and she put her arm around his shoulders.

"I've been so mean to her lately. I wish I hadn't been so mean," he muttered, never taking his red-rimmed eyes off Pekin.

"Yeah. What was wrong with you? Pekin couldn't figure out what she did wrong and was upset that you were mad at her. She didn't know how to fix it. So, why?"

"Because! Because of Allen Torkelson. That's why. I hated that she was going out with someone else."

"You mean…you like her?"

"Of course I like her. She's my best friend, but, I don't know, it's like my feelings for her have changed. I was jealous." He still hadn't looked away from Pekin.

"You dope. Then why didn't you tell her?"

"She probably thinks of me as a brother. I mean, we're *buddies*. How do you change from that?"

"*You* apparently did. And *she* thinks you think of *her* as a sister. God. You two need an interpreter. If we get her back…*when* we get her back, you have to tell her. At least let her know she didn't do anything wrong. And what was your deal with Vanessa Dooley?"

"Now isn't the time for that," Mildew said, shaking her head at Amber and Scout. "I'm going to say a prayer of protection for all of us. Anyone who wants to pray with me, please do. I'm going to ask for spiritual protection so that George Trent can't harm any of us."

She closed her eyes and raised her hands upward, then prayed for the rescuers to be bathed in white light and protected from evil in any form. She asked for help removing the entity from Pekin, and said a prayer of thanks." She opened her eyes and lowered her hands.

Pekin glared at Mildew with hatred as the little woman approached. Before Mildew could speak, George Trent started to laugh. Threats and foul language poured out of poor Pekin's mouth.

"You haven't met the likes of me before," Mildew said calmly.

The nasty grin faded from the haunted face.

"Yes, I believe you will leave our Pekin. You don't belong here."

Curses again poured out of Pekin's mouth. "Not likely. She's mine now," growled the unearthly voice.

Scout and Amber watched. Pekin's parents stood clutching each other, Melissa's face buried in her husband's shoulder.

Time passed. The creature held tight to its innocent victim. Mildew glanced over her shoulder. "Scout, in my bag. Find the salt and sprinkle it in front of the door. If the ghost comes out, it cannot be allowed to leave this room."

Scout scrambled to his feet and did as instructed. When he was done, Scout didn't return to his spot on the ground. Instead, he approached Mildew.

"He won't let her go."

"He will. In time."

"I need to talk to Pekin. I don't know if I'll have another chance. Please."

He jumped as the police pounded on the door, demanding to be let in. Nervous glances passed among the group.

Scout still looked at Mildew, and after a moment she nodded and stepped aside.

He knelt in front of the thrashing entity, ignoring the filth pouring from her innocent mouth, and stared into the angry, rage-filled eyes that weren't the eyes of his best friend. He wanted to take hold of her, to grab her and make her listen, but knew he shouldn't get that close. Pekin wouldn't hurt him, but this entity would certainly do its best to cause as much damage as it was capable of.

"Pekin," he said, shaking off the distraction of the pounding on the door. "Pekin, it's me. Scout. You have to fight. I know you're still in there. I know you want him to let you go. You have to *fight*. Fight for your parents, your friends. Hell, Pekin, fight for *me*, even if I don't deserve it. I treated you badly. I shouldn't have been mean to you. You have to let me tell you how sorry I am. You have to let me make it better."

The ghost roared and lunged at Scout, causing him to rock back on his heels. "She's not here, you pitiful nothing. She'll never be here. You can't make me leave." The ghost started babbling nonsense, trying to drown out Scout's words. An old rusty lantern, forgotten in a corner of the room, flew through the air and bashed Scout in the head. Amber shrieked and scrambled to his side. A trickle of blood appeared at his hairline, growing heavier almost immediately and running in rivulets down his forehead, blurring his eyesight. He rubbed his eyes, pulling up his T-shirt to wipe the blood from his eyes. He could hear Amber calling his name, but her voice seemed far off. He shook his head, trying to clear his thoughts, as George Trent's booming, evil laughter filled his ears.

Scout bravely pulled himself together and started pleading with Pekin again. Suddenly the entity seemed distracted.

Pekin, amid the noise emitting from the cotton ball in her head, heard the voice of her adored Scout. She struggled to hear him, struggled to push back on the pressure that trapped her in that little corner of her mind. His words were amazing and, more than that, they gave her the courage to summon every ounce of strength she could muster.

"I was jealous, Pekin. I don't want Allen to be your boyfriend. *I* want to be your boyfriend. That's why I need you to come back. Come back to me, Pekie."

Pekin summoned a psychic strength she hadn't known she possessed, drawing in her breath until her imaginary cheeks were bursting, and blew it out with all the force she could manage straight at the obstruction in her head. She saw it blasted out of her head. Exhaustion hit her like a rock and, she fainted.

"He's out," Mildew shouted as the room grew cold and a wind swirled through the small space. "And he's mad. We need to get out of here."

Scout picked Pekin up as Mildew unlocked the storage room door. When he swayed, his face ghastly pale beneath the blood still oozing from his wound, Edward stepped forward and took Pekin from his arms, shouting for Amber to help Scout. She scooted under Scout's arm as his legs buckled. Melissa took his other side, her arm around his waist, and, between them, they pushed their way past the officers gathering on the stairs. Before the police could barge in, Mildew turned and shook more salt onto the floor in front of the door, making sure there were no breaks in the line. She pulled the door shut and followed everyone up the stairs and out of the cramped passageway.

"Call for an ambulance," Officer Elliott shouted orders to his officers. "And don't any of you leave," he said to Pekin's rescuers.

"WHAT'S WRONG WITH HER?" Melissa asked in alarm as Pekin lay unresponsive on the sofa in the parlor where Edward had placed her. He backed away to make room for Melissa to kneel beside the unconscious girl.

"She's been through a lot and is most likely exhausted beyond belief. She'll be okay after she's had a chance to rest," Mildew said.

Scout sat on the floor, his back against one of the chairs, his head in his hands, while Amber attempted to look at his bloody head wounds. Mildew had found a clean towel among her traveling supplies and after dampening it she wiped at his face.

"Scout, you did it," Amber said, gingerly resting her arm across his shoulders in a careful hug. "You brought her back."

He turned his head to look at her, wincing at the sharp pain. "I didn't do anything but talk to her," he said. "I just told her to——"

"You told her to fight. And she *did*," Mildew said. "I didn't think she was strong enough to expel the ghost, but young love came through."

"Young love?" Scout asked, climbing to his feet.

"I'd say that's the clearest example of young love I've ever seen," Mildew said with a smile. "Congratulations, young man. I think you have yourself a girlfriend."

"That's so great!" Amber gushed. "You and Pekin. I *love* it."

Scout sank into the chair in a daze. When he felt a hand on his shoulder, he looked up.

"Thanks for what you did back there. We owe you for bringing our daughter back to us," Mr. Dewlap said, extending his hand.

Scout blinked, then shook Edward's hand. "I…just wanted her back."

"We all did, son. You saved her. Thank you." He clapped Scout's shoulder again. "Are you okay? All that blood——"

"I'm…it's nothing. I'm just glad Pekin's okay. She is, isn't she?" A worried look crossed his face.

"I certainly hope so. When the paramedics get here, we'll know more. At the very least, however, that monster doesn't have her anymore."

CHAPTER THIRTY-FIVE

~~~~~~

SCOUT GLANCED TOWARD THE FRONT DOOR at the sound of sirens. He walked out onto the porch, then stood aside as the ambulance attendants wheeled a gurney into the house. He begged off when one of the attendants tried to look at his head wound, but the attendant pulled him out and sat him down in the back of the ambulance to begin cleaning out the injury. "You need some stitches for that," the EMT said.

"Just take care of my friend," Scout said. "I promise I'll go to the ER after you take care of her."

The EMT shrugged and applied gauze and a bandage to Scout's head. He examined Scout's eyes and asked whether he was experiencing any lightheadedness or felt faint. Satisfied that Scout probably hadn't suffered a concussion, he said, "Okay. Just be sure you follow up with your doctor. Otherwise, you risk infection and will have a nasty scar."

Scout hurried back to Pekin as the EMTs checked her pulse and raised her lids to shine a light in her eyes. Within moments she was lifted onto the gurney and being loaded into the ambulance. Melissa climbed into the back as Edward headed for his car to meet them at the hospital.

Officer Elliott approached Scout, Amber, and Mildew and stood, feet apart, hands on hips, looking every inch the authority he was.

"Officer—," Mildew started.

"Save it, Willingham. I had a chat with Detective Burroughs. He vouched for you and said we should drop the matter, especially now that it seems the victim is going to be okay. But, I don't usually look the other way. Watch it."

"I will, Officer Elliott. Thanks for being understanding."

He huffed, turned and walked out the door.

The three rescuers plopped onto the sofa.

"What the *hell* happened down there?" Scout asked, shaking his head, then grabbing it to stop the splitting headache sparking behind his eyes.

"Can he get out?" Amber asked fearfully.

"No. I think he's safe down there. But we're not done. We have to help Miranda cross over. Then we can worry about what to do with George Trent." She looked at Scout. "That pretty much *was* hell, wasn't it?"

SCOUT AND AMBER CAMPED OUT in the hospital's waiting room chairs until visiting hours were over, then Amber's parents gave them a ride home.

Pekin's parents were both in the room with their daughter. After loads of medical tests, the doctor said they needed to observe her overnight, but it was possible she would be released before noon the following day.

Melissa sat at Pekin's bedside, stroking her daughter's hair. She'd insisted on staying in the room, having convinced Edward to go home and get some sleep. Once or twice during the night, a nightmare disturbed Pekin's sleep. She whimpered and thrashed until her mother was able to soothe her back into an uneasy slumber.

Once Pekin was back home, her mother insisted she stay in bed the rest of the day, and Pekin had been too exhausted to argue.

Both Amber and Scout called to check on her. Melissa reassured them she was doing as well as could be expected but needed time to process what she'd gone through at Elmwood. "She might be up for a visit tomorrow," she offered.

Pekin shuffled into the kitchen the next morning, the aroma of pancakes and bacon floating up the stairs more than she could resist. She was a sight. Flannel pajamas and fuzzy slippers, wrapped in a blanket despite the sun shining warmly through the kitchen window.

Tears sprang to Melissa's eyes as her daughter slumped onto a chair. She gave Pekin a quick hug and placed a glass of orange juice on the table in front of her, followed by a plate of pancakes and bacon.

"How are you feeling this morning, dear?" she asked.

Pekin shrugged, not looking up from her plate.

"If you want to talk about what happened—"

Edward and Campbell chose that moment to arrive in the kitchen, and Melissa went back to the stove to flip over the pancakes that were bubbling on the griddle. "It'll be just a minute," she said over her shoulder.

Edward cleared his throat and touched a hand to his cheek, looking awkward. Pekin glanced up and offered a weak smile before turning her attention back to her breakfast. He made a couple of half-hearted attempts to draw her out, but she was withdrawn and seemed reluctant to talk.

"I'm off today, honey," he said to her. "In case, you know, you need anything."

"Thanks, Dad," she offered, briefly glancing up at him.

She knew her family wanted to talk about what happened, but the words didn't come fast or easily. Her responses were mostly one syllable. The previous day's events had drained her of all energy.

Even Campbell cut back on her sarcasm and showed genuine concern for the somber girl her sister had become.

Sniffling, Campbell bent and gave her sister a hug. "I'm so glad you're home, Pekie. Please be okay. I'm so worried."

"I'm fine. Really. You don't need to worry. I'm just kinda tired."

"I have to go to work or I'd stick around, but I'll see you tonight, okay?"

Pekin smiled at her sister. "See you then."

She carried her plate to the sink and rinsed it.

"Leave it, honey," her mother said. "I'll take care of the dishes."

"Okay," Pekin said, and shuffled toward the door.

"Are you going back to bed?"

"No. I really want a shower."

"I'm sure you'll feel much better afterward," Melissa said. "Call if you need me."

Her parents were in the family room when Pekin came back downstairs. She curled up against her father on the sofa, who put a tender arm around her. "Your friends are coming over soon. You up to it?"

"I'm okay, Dad." They sat like that watching TV until Melissa announced the arrival of Amber and Scout.

Edward kissed Pekin on the head and stood up. "I'll be in my office if you need anything," he said.

Amber burst into the den with a cheerful hello and bent to hug Pekin, who looked frail and a little distant. "For you," Amber said, handing Pekin the mocha she'd picked up for her friend from Starbucks.

"It's so good to have you back! We were so scared."

"You guys were wonderful," Pekin said. She took a sip of the mocha, and set the cup on the coffee table.

"Aww, it was nothing," Amber kidded, then looked closer at her friend. "You okay?"

"I'm fine," Pekin said tiredly.

Scout mumbled a greeting, but wouldn't look at Pekin. "Glad you're home," he said.

"Scout, what's wrong with you? Why are you so low key? Pekin's *back*. You *saved* her," Amber scolded.

"I—" he shuffled his feet, his head down.

"Scout," Pekin said quietly, extending her hand to him.

He looked up when she spoke, then took her hand. She pulled him down next to her on the couch. Neither one spoke for a minute, as Amber watched, dumbfounded. "You guys," she said in exasperation.

Pekin looked at Scout, and threw her arms around his neck. "I don't know what to say," she said. "Thank you seems so lame."

He rested his head on her shoulder for a moment, then hugged her tightly. "Thank God you're okay," he said.

"So, you guys," Amber said. "You're in love!"

"Oh my *God*, Amber," Scout said in horror.

"Well, you are," she said in her defense.

Pekin smiled.

Scout still looked uncomfortable. Pekin slid her hand into his and gave it an encouraging squeeze. He glanced at her and smiled, a small smile. He seemed embarrassed, and Amber watching their every move didn't help.

Pekin knew she wasn't her old self. She was somber and distant. Even Amber's teasing hadn't brought more than a tired smile to her face.

Melissa stuck her head in to see if anyone needed anything. Scout got up and followed her into the kitchen.

"Is she okay?" he asked.

Melissa took a moment to answer. "She will be. She's been through a trauma. She needs time to process what happened to her."

"I hate seeing her so…not Pekin."

"I know," Melissa said, putting a hand on his arm. "She's gonna really need you guys to help her through this."

He gave her a shaky smile and wandered back to the den, taking a seat next to Pekin.

"How are you doing?" he asked as he put his hand over hers. "I mean, are you really okay?"

"I'm fine. Why does everyone keep asking me that?"

"You know why. You're not you, Pekie."

"And I wasn't me for a while back there, was I?" she responded, a slight edge to her voice.

"No, you weren't. And we got you back. But it seems like not completely."

"I'm sorry. I'm just…I guess I'm still freaked out. You can't imagine what it's like to have no control over yourself. To watch yourself trying to hurt your friends, to say awful things. And you can't make it stop, no matter how hard you try."

"No, I can't imagine it," he said, picking up her hand and clasping it in both of his. "What was it like? You know, when he took you?"

When she didn't answer immediately, he said, "You don't have to talk about it if you aren't ready."

"No. It's all right." She shivered as her mind returned to that memory. "I was scared, Scout. I was so cold. He showed me what he did to Miranda. He touched my forehead and these awful pictures came into my head. I *saw* him carrying Miranda out the backdoor and pushing open the door to the garden shed. I felt it when he choked her. I *was* her."

Scout didn't say anything as he watched her, waiting for her to continue at her own pace.

She snuggled closer to him. "You're so warm," she said. "I didn't think I'd ever be warm again."

He put an arm around her shoulders and rubbed her arm. "Do you want a blanket? I can go—"

"No. This is nice. I'm okay."

"When he...when you...when you weren't you—"

"I must have been unconscious. Maybe I could have kept him out if I—"

"He was really powerful, Pekie. I don't think you could have stopped him."

"I could hear you talking to me and I wanted to answer you but he wouldn't let me. All I could do was watch." Pekin dropped her eyes. "Scout, did you mean it, those things you said when I was...*wasn't* me? About—"

"I meant every word, Pekie. I'm sorry. I know we're just friends, and maybe you don't think of me—"

"I thought you didn't think of *me* that way. I've liked you for so long, and there was Vanessa Dooley—"

"Vanessa Dooley? I don't like Vanessa Dooley. I like *you*."

"But she—"

"She isn't my type," he said with a grin. "She isn't you."

"Oh, my God," Amber said. "*Finally*."

Chapter Thirty-Six

~~~~~~

"YOU SHOULD HAVE SEEN MILDEW," Amber piped up, trying to steer the conversation in a safer direction.

"Mildew?" Pekin asked, confused.

"Yes, Mildew. You remember her from when she dropped in on us at Elmwood to see if we needed help? Well, it turned out we did need her help. And Miranda's. Miranda told us where to find you." Amber's voice reflected her excitement.

"What happened to you back there," Scout said. "If Mildew hadn't—"

"I don't want to talk about it anymore," Pekin responded. "Do you mind?"

"Of course not," Scout said. "I just thought it might help to get it out."

She looked down at her hands, then up at him. "Tell me what happened."

"What?" Scout looked at her in confusion.

"You mean what *we* did?" Amber asked.

"Yes."

As Amber and Scout took turns recounting the events, Pekin was silent, taking it all in.

"Miranda told us where to find you. You should have seen your dad," Amber said. "He went 'Whoa!' when he saw Miranda for himself. Before that he was mad because he thought we were making stuff up."

"Cool. Wish I could have seen that," Pekin said, for the first time a glimmer of her old self peeking through.

When they were mostly done filling her in, Pekin shivered. "He showed me what he did to Miranda. I felt what he did to her like I was there. It was horrific." She paused. "And Miranda wasn't the only one."

"Wait. What?" Scout's mouth fell open.

"There were others, before. Three other girls. They were never found, either."

"He told you that?" Scout asked.

"He *showed* me. He made me be them and feel everything they felt."

"Oh, my God," Amber gasped. "Miranda said he could scare you to death." Amber looked at Pekin in horror. Pekin looked back, her eyes haunted.

No one spoke. Scout pulled Pekin into his arms, and she started to cry, softly at first and then great hiccupping sobs racked her body.

He held her until he felt the shaking subside. When she had regained control, Scout let her go. "We don't need to talk about this anymore," he said gently.

"There's one more thing." She paused. "I know where Miranda is."

"Is she in the shed?"

"Yes. There's a trap door, and he covered it with bags of fertilizer and leaves. That's where he left her."

"Why did he come back and haunt her? I mean, wasn't he old when he died?" Amber asked.

"No, actually," Pekin said. "His missing finger, the stump of his finger, got infected from the dirt and germs in the shed, and he died a couple of months later. He blamed Miranda for trapping him at Elmwood."

"Wow," Scout said, shaking his head. "What do we do now?"

"Call the police?" Pekin asked. "Do you think they'll do anything?"

"What about Mildew?" Amber asked.

"What about her?" Pekin asked, confused.

"Should we call her? Maybe she can help us talk to the police."

"I guess so. And I need to thank her for…everything," Pekin said.

"Are you up to it this afternoon?" Scout asked. "Or would you rather wait."

"I want to get everything over with. Let's just do it."

AMBER ANSWERED THE DOOR when Mildew arrived and showed her into the den.

Mildew went straight to Pekin. "My dear, I'm so glad to see you doing so well." She extended her hand.

Pekin looked at her appraisingly, and offered her hand in return, which Mildew squeezed warmly.

"So," Mildew said, glancing around. "What's going on?"

"Before we start," Pekin said, "I have to thank you for all you did yesterday. Amber and Scout said they couldn't have done it without you."

"I'm glad I was able to help, but your friends were every bit as brave. Amber stole more Holy Water, and Scout...Scout's voice led you back. He made you fight. Actually, you saved yourself. You're a very brave young lady."

"Still, if you hadn't found me when you did—"

"Miranda had a hand in that," Amber added. "You would have been proud of her. You know how shy she is? She *still* came out and told us how to find you. In front of *five* people. And two of them were strangers."

"Is Miranda okay? Where is she?"

Amber pulled the black velvet pouch out of her pocket. "I've been keeping her safe for you."

"She should be here for this, too, shouldn't she? If we find her body, she'll be crossing over. I think she should know."

Chapter Thirty-Seven

"BRING HER OUT," AMBER SAID, her eyes lighting up in excitement.

Pekin opened the bag and slipped the ring on her finger. Griselda, who'd been dozing on the ottoman, arched her back, hair bristling everywhere, and hissed as she dashed from the room.

Miranda's shimmer appeared, then she was fully present. She seemed confused.

What is happening? she asked.

When Miranda noticed Pekin, the ghost smiled. *You're free. I'm so glad.*

"Thank you for helping to find me."

Why am I here? Where is he?

"That's one reason I summoned you. I've told Amber and Scout about what happened in the cellar. Now, I want to tell the rest of you. And, Miranda, this will impact you the most. When we find your...body, you'll be free to go into the light."

Miranda didn't respond, and after a pause Pekin recounted her story, although she played down the horror she'd endured at George Trent's hands. When she was finished with the retelling, Pekin slumped onto the sofa, exhausted. Once again, her eyes looked haunted. No one spoke, overwhelmed by the weight of what they'd learned.

After a moment, Mildew patted her arm. "What you endured, I'm so glad it's over. As awful as it was, you now have the ability to help Miranda move on. And you'll be able to bring peace to three other families."

"It's been a hundred years, there's probably no one left to care about those poor girls."

"Not true. Families pass stories down through the generations.

Don't you think the mystery of a stolen child would be a part of a family's history? Maybe the child's parents and siblings have passed, but there are generations living on. They will appreciate knowing the end of the story."

"Do you know the names of the other girls, or where he left their bodies?" Scout asked.

"I know their names. I have a general idea of where they are. He threw them down an old well on land where the Trents had a summer house. Do you think that will help?"

"We know all this stuff, but what good will it do? The police didn't believe anything we told them. They're not going to believe this either," Amber said.

"Amber's right. What good would it do? The police will think you're nuts. They'll think we're all nuts," Scout said.

"I might be able to help here," Mildew said. "I have a working relationship with the Springdale Police Department. I've helped Captain Burroughs in the past. He'll listen."

"Can you call him?"

"I will do that. He'll probably want you to go down to the station to give your statement."

"Can't he come here?" Scout asked. "Pekin's been through so much already. I think she'd be more comfortable here. I don't want her to be any more stressed out than she already is."

"I'll see what I can do. Maybe the thought of solving a very old cold case will be reward enough to get him to talk to us."

I didn't know about the others, Miranda said suddenly.

Everyone looked at her. *I thought I was the only one.*

"It's probably good that you didn't know. There was nothing you could do anyway," Pekin said.

"If Miranda crosses over, what happens to George Trent's ghost?" Scout asked. "Will he still be trapped in that room? What if someone accidentally lets him out?"

Pekin shuddered.

"I've been thinking about that," Mildew said. "I don't mean to sound indelicate, but remember that Miranda bit off his finger and swallowed it."

Miranda looked down and smoothed the skirt of her dress.

"The police will take the finger bone. That's how they can confirm that George Trent was the murderer," Mildew said. "But, if we can get the finger back when they're done with it—"

"Do you think they'll give it back?" Scout asked. "On the ghost shows Pekin always has us watching, there are laws governing disposal of human remains."

"Hmm, that is true," Mildew said, looking thoughtful.

"Can you, like, put a spell on the bone or something?" Amber asked.

"I don't do spells, Amber. Sorry. But maybe if we soak it in Holy Water and then insist that it be cremated..."

"Or, maybe, is there some process you could do before they take away the remains?" Scout asked.

"Would the cops let us anywhere near the remains?" Pekin asked.

"Probably not," Mildew said.

"What if...this is just a thought, but what if we go get the finger bone before we call the cops? If we were careful, maybe we could do whatever you need to do and then put it back where we found it?" Scout looked at Mildew questioningly.

"How would we even recognize a finger bone?" Amber asked.

"I wish I'd paid more attention in my anatomy class," he said.

"Me, too," Amber said. "Oh wait. I haven't taken it yet."

"Kids, listen," Mildew interrupted. "It depends on the position of the body." She shot a look at Miranda. "I'm sorry we're discussing you like this, Miranda. Would you rather not be here?"

Miranda shook her head. *I know my body is lying in the dark somewhere. The body isn't me. It's no longer me, I mean. I want to stay.*

"Unfortunately," Mildew continued, "I doubt we could pick it out from a jumble of bones."

"Not to mention," Pekin added, "think how much dust and dirt will be covering them. It would be hard to search through the bones without disturbing them because they'll probably be unrecognizable through all the dirt."

"I vote against disturbing the bones," Amber said. "It's creepy, and we'd be interfering with a crime scene. It could be illegal. Since, you know, it's a crime scene."

"I hadn't thought of that," said Scout, frowning.

"Do you suppose, if your police captain comes here to take my statement, that if we could show him Miranda and if we took him to the secret room and he could experience the pissed-off ghost, he might be willing to help us?" Pekin asked.

She turned to Miranda. "Would you be willing to appear to the policeman? It's important that he believes us."

Miranda looked apprehensive.

"Look, Miranda, you've come all this way. You're in a room full of people. Would you ever have thought that could happen? Just one more person. That's all we need. You're going to be free to move on anyway, but do you want George to be able to keep haunting your house? *I* don't want him to still exist there. Please, Miranda? I don't think I'll ever feel safe until he's gone."

Miranda nodded silently.

"Thanks," Pekin said. "I'd hug you if I could."

Miranda smiled at her.

"Anyway, Mildew, what do you think?"

Mildew said "hmm" and narrowed her eyes in thought. "Captain Burroughs has always had to take on faith whatever I've told him. I think he might be more willing to help us out if he saw what the stakes are. I'll see what I can do."

"I think Pekin has had enough visiting for one day," said Melissa, who'd been watching the proceedings from the doorway of the den. "Mildew, let us know what you find out. Scout and Amber, maybe you can come back to see her tomorrow. She has to be exhausted."

"Pekin, you look worn out," Scout said, standing. "I think we've done enough for today. You should rest."

"Yeah, I am a little worn out. Miranda, I'm going to take off the ring, now. Is that okay with you?"

She nodded silently and vanished when Pekin put the ring back in the velvet pouch. Pekin closed her eyes and dreamed of taking George down.

Chapter Thirty-Eight

"WE'D LIKE TO TELL YOU what happened first, if you don't mind, and then you can ask questions," Pekin said. She was ensconced on the sofa between her Scout and Amber.

Captain Burroughs looked skeptical. "That's not usually how we do it."

"Maybe not, but humor me. It's going to be hard for you to accept a lot of what you hear, but what Mildew told you and what I'm telling you is the truth. If you don't hear the whole story, you won't understand."

"We'll start with that. Officer Elliott is here as well. He witnessed some of what happened."

"You took quite a chunk out of my shoulder," Officer Elliott said to Pekin. "That's assaulting an officer, in case you were wondering."

"I...I what?" Pekin asked. "I bit you?"

"You know you bit me," he said evenly.

"I'm sorry. But it wasn't me."

"I'm pretty sure it wasn't anyone else," he said.

"That's enough," Captain Burroughs said, raising a hand. "This isn't getting us anywhere." He turned back to Pekin, "Okay. Shoot."

"I know you're going to have a hard time believing this," she said, looking nervous. "But Mildew said you have experience with her, so here goes. Amber, Scout and I started a business of helping ghosts cross over." She ignored the eye rolls. "12 Elmwood was our first case."

From there, Pekin described meeting the owner of the Elmwood house and being told the story of Miranda, who was kidnapped at 14 and never found. The owner, Elonia Collins, believed that the house was haunted and wanted the ghost gone.

"We decided immediately it had to be Miranda who was haunting the house," Pekin said. "We found out we were right. After several visits, we got Miranda to appear to us. She told us what happened to her and we figured out who did it. She didn't know where her body was and we needed to find it in order for her to cross over. From what Miranda remembered of that day, we decided she must be in the garden shed in the backyard. We managed to get her out of the house because she said she wasn't alone there and she was afraid, so we left her in the car."

"You left a ghost in the car. What? Sitting in the passenger seat?" Officer Elliott scoffed.

"No. She is actually attached to a ring, and when we took the ring out of the house she came with it. So we left the ring in the car because she was afraid."

She looked at Scout for help.

"We went to Elmwood meaning to go to the shed and see if we could find Miranda's body, but while we were in the house, another ghost accosted us," Scout said. "We knew who it was. George Trent. He was a neighbor of the Talberts and he's the one who killed Miranda. Anyway, George was furious and throwing things around. We all sprayed him with Holy Water that Amber stole from St. Michael's—"

"Scout! I can't believe you ratted me out!" Amber cried.

"It's okay, Amber. I'm pretty sure it isn't a crime to take the Holy Water. Anyway, when we sprayed him he went ballistic and grabbed Pekin. I tried to save her but he threw me into a wall and escaped with her. We looked all over the house, and then we called Mildew and we all looked again but didn't have any luck. Then Pekin's parents and the police showed up. They looked all over the house, too, but they didn't have any better luck than we did."

"Captain, you're not buying this, are you? They got us to let them do another search and they went right to her. They had her all tied up. When I tried to help the victim, she bit me. And then they locked us out of the room until they were ready to come out. This is all bullshit."

"Watch your language, Officer Elliott," Capital Burroughs said. "Let them finish their story." He turned to Scout. "How *did* you know where to find her?"

"We didn't. But we thought Miranda might know, since she'd been in that house with George for so long. She's the one who told us about the hidden passage and the storage room."

Officer Elliott rolled his eyes again, barely containing his irritation.

"Mildew, why don't you tell what happened then?" Scout said.

"I'm happy to. Captain, Officer." She nodded at them. "I realized the ghost wasn't going to let us walk in and take Pekin, so we came prepared. When I opened the door to the storage room, the ghost rushed us, so I sprayed him with Holy Water." She winked at Amber. "George was furious, and that's when he entered Pekin."

"What do you mean, *entered* her?" Captain Burroughs asked.

"Took over her body. Like a possession. That's why we had to restrain her, so she couldn't hurt herself or others. Apparently, you found out the hard way, Officer Elliott, what a possessed person can do."

Captain Burroughs again put up a hand to warn Officer Elliott to hold his tongue. "So, how did you get him to come out?"

"Actually, Scout did that. I believe he and the victim have feelings for each other, and he begged her to fight back. For him. And she did."

Pekin blushed, afraid to look at Scout.

"And that's the whole story," Mildew concluded.

"Yes, well——" Captain Burroughs started.

"And one more thing, Captain," Mildew said. "While George Trent controlled Pekin's body, he showed her things, horrible things. He showed her where to find Miranda's body. He also showed her three other victims. All girls like Miranda. George turned out to be a serial killer. Pekin has the names and approximate location of the other girls."

Captain Burroughs sighed.

Officer Elliott took advantage of the pause in the story. "That's the most preposterous thing I've ever heard. I think this whole thing is a hoax. I'm not sure what the purpose was, but *no one* is going to buy that load of crap."

Chapter Thirty-Nine

"**W**E'RE PREPARED TO OFFER PROOF," Mildew said.

"What kind of proof?" the Captain asked.

"I'll tell you, but, first, there's something we need you to do for us."

"Which is?"

"Pekin?" Mildew turned to her.

Pekin, who'd been leaning against Scout, sat up straight. "When George Trent was assaulting Miranda, before he killed her, she bit off part of his finger and swallowed it. We believe that's why he's trapped here. After you've examined the remains, we'd like the finger bone back. Mildew needs it to banish George's ghost from the house."

Officer Elliott threw up his hands in frustration, a look of pure disbelief on his face.

"That's unorthodox," Captain Burroughs said.

"Is anything about this case orthodox?" Mildew asked.

"So. Your proof?"

"Yes, our proof. Captain, you and I have collaborated before, but up until now you've had to take my word for whatever I've told you. Because these cases are so old, my word may not be enough, so Miranda has agreed to meet you."

"You have *got* to be kidding me," Officer Elliott sputtered.

"I'm actually *not* kidding you, Officer Elliott," Mildew said. "Are you saying you wouldn't believe your own eyes?"

"Hey. I can be open-minded. Go on. Blow my socks off."

She glanced at Captain Burroughs. "Are you ready?"

"I am. I have to say I'm skeptical, but if you can prove to me that ghosts actually exist, well, it will be an interesting experience."

Pekin took the black pouch out of her pocket and put the ring on her finger. "Miranda, can you come out? I told you there would be one stranger. There are actually two, but they're both police officers. They're having a hard time believing our story. You're the only one they might believe. It's almost over, Miranda. Please do this for us…for yourself."

Nothing happened for a moment, and Officer Elliott's face reflected his certainty that nothing *would* happen. Pekin shivered as a chill descended on the room. Then there was a shimmer and Mildew pointed at it. In the next moment, the petite blonde girl in an old-fashioned taffeta dress stood in their midst.

Hello, her ghostly voice said.

Officer Elliott's mouth dropped open, and there was awe on the Captain's face.

Would you like to take my statement? Miranda asked the Captain.

Too stunned to speak, he stared until Mildew nudged him. "Captain?"

"Yes, sorry," he stammered. He flipped his notebook to a new page. "I'm Captain Burroughs. You must be Miranda Talbert."

Yes, she nodded.

"I'm ready when you are."

As Miranda spoke, now and then the Captain would interject a question, which Miranda did her best to answer. When she was finished, Captain Burroughs clicked the button on his pen and closed his notebook.

Officer Elliott, who'd been mostly silent during Miranda's statement, said, "I owe you all an apology. I didn't believe a word you said. And I certainly didn't believe in *ghosts*. But you're *here*," he said to Miranda. "I don't even know what to say. I'm just really…I'm honored to meet you, Miss Talbert."

Miranda smiled sweetly at him, doing a small curtsy. *And I'm honored to meet you, too, Officer Elliott.*

"What's it like? You know, being dead?" he asked tactlessly.

"What the hell?" Scout said.

It's okay, Miranda said to Scout. Then she addressed Officer Elliott. *For me, sometimes it was peaceful. And lonely. But he was there, too. Sometimes I was afraid. Very afraid. When he was bored, he would torment me.* She sighed. *I was used to my life, used to being alone mostly. Then Pekin and her friends came. They made it fun for me. I love them*, she said shyly.

"We love you, too," Amber said, putting her hand to her mouth as tears started in her eyes.

"Before everyone gets too mushy," Captain Burroughs said, "I'm going to arrange to meet a forensics team at Elmwood this afternoon. Let's see if we can find...you," he said to Miranda.

Can I go now?, the ghost asked Pekin.

"Of course," Pekin said. "After we get you back, we'll talk again. Mildew will help us figure out what we do then to help set you free. Thank you for everything, Miranda. And Amber spoke for us all. We *do* love you."

She slipped the ring off her finger and put it back in the pouch.

Captain Burroughs and Officer Elliott looked in confusion at the spot where Miranda had stood only a moment before. "I wish I'd recorded that statement," he said, shaking his head.

"I'm not sure it would work," Pekin said. "We took pictures of Miranda at Elmwood and you could see all of us in the pictures, but later Miranda faded from the photo. The same thing would probably happen to your recording."

"Huh. Maybe you're right." Captain Burroughs pulled out his phone and made arrangements for the afternoon.

"I assume you all want to be there when we search the shed?" he asked.

"We do," Pekin said.

Chapter Forty

PEKIN WAS AFRAID. After unlocking the door at 12 Elmwood, she was reluctant to go inside. "You don't have to go in there, you know," Amber offered. "I'll stay out here with you."

"Yeah. We can take the cops out to the shed. You can wait in the car," Scout said.

Taking a deep breath, she said, "No, I should be there." But she hesitated.

"It'll be okay, dear," Mildew said. "George is locked up in the basement. He can't get you. But don't feel you have to go in. You have every reason to skip this part."

Pekin looked at Scout for support. Her stomach was tied in knots. *What if Mildew was wrong?* Still, she squared her shoulders in determination.

"She's fine," Scout said, taking Pekin's hand. He looked at her. "We got this."

Pekin squeezed his hand, and went through the door with him, hand in hand. Before she could think about being afraid, or about the fact that the boy of her dreams was holding her hand, two police cruisers pulled up in front of the house, followed by a black SUV and a forensics van.

Scout turned and stepped outside, followed by Pekin, so that he could direct the forensics team to park in the alley in back, then went inside to get the key and unlock the gate for them. He was back at Pekin's side within moments, resting an arm around her shoulders.

Captain Burroughs got out of the SUV. "Shall we?" he said, and headed inside.

Mildew and Amber led the way down the hall to the backdoor. It was hard to miss the unearthly voice bellowing from somewhere behind the walls of the hallway, shouting threats and curses.

"What the hell?" Captain Burroughs said.

Mildew nodded toward the sound. "That's George for you."

The officers exchanged a glance, then followed Mildew into the yard. The door to the shed was already open and the team from the van was taking photos of the interior.

Scout offered to help remove the debris on the floor so they could search for the trapdoor, but the forensics team asked him to stay back, so he had to be content with watching. It took a few minutes before one of the investigators announced that the trapdoor had been found. Scout moved from the doorway so the forensics team could climb down into the cramped space in the floor. Almost as soon as the door was pulled open, a voice shouted that they'd located what looked like human remains.

Scout gave Pekin and Amber high fives. "We did it. We found Miranda," he said, pulling his friends into a group hug. "Yeah," he said softly. "We did it."

He glanced over his shoulder at the investigators milling around the shed. "I was more than a little nervous they wouldn't find anything."

"We should tell her," Amber said. "Miranda. We need to tell her."

Chapter Forty-One

~~~~~~

HOURS LATER, the forensics team lowered a black body bag through the trap door and, shortly after, it was carefully lifted out of the hole.

Mildew approached Captain Burroughs. "Remember what I asked you?" she said.

"Refresh my memory," he responded.

"About the bit of finger Miranda swallowed. I asked if we could have it."

"I don't see that happening. The finger is evidence. The scales of justice move at a snail's pace in these old cases. Even if I said you could have it, it would be years before you could take it."

"Can I borrow it then?" she persisted.

"Borrow it?"

"Yes. If I have it, maybe I can con George into crossing over. I need leverage."

"Look, it's not like I can unzip the bag and pull out a finger. There are a ton of bones in that bag. I don't know if they're in one piece or not. It's gonna take forensics a long time before they can sort out the skeleton and discover if there's one small bone fragment left over. I just don't know how we would do that."

Mildew looked thoughtful. She excused herself and started poking around the garden and along the fence. No one spoke as they watched her, curious what she was doing. She picked up objects and tossed them aside for several minutes, then popped upright with a smile. When she joined the group again she held up an old dirty root. "Is this about the size, do you think?"

"For a finger bone, you mean?" Scout asked. He held up his hand beside it to measure the width. "Could be."

"I have an idea," Mildew said. "Maybe we don't need the fingertip after all."

Addressing Captain Burroughs, she said, "You've seen one ghost now. Want to see another?"

He looked over his shoulder toward the house then back at Mildew. "The murderer?"

"Yes. The murderer. The monster. Whatever you want to call him. I'm going to bluff him and hope he takes the bait. Who wants in?"

"I...I don't think I can," Pekin said in a small voice.

"Amber, have you got any Holy Water left?" Mildew asked.

"Um, I think so. I didn't use all mine so it should still be in my backpack."

"Can you go get it, please?"

"Sure," Amber said, and headed for the house.

"I should still have some salt around here," Mildew said.

"You're not going in the room with him again, are you?" Pekin asked in horror.

"I'm hoping I won't have to. There's salt along the doorway so he can't come out. I can talk to him through the open door." She rubbed her hands together in glee. "I'm going to enjoy this."

Amber showed up with her spray bottle of Holy Water and handed it to Mildew.

"Okay. Who's in?" Mildew looked around at everyone watching her intently.

"I'm game," Captain Burroughs said.

"Me, too," Officer Elliott said.

"Me," Amber said.

"Me," Scout said, then looked at Pekin, who shrank back.

"I don't think I can go in there. I'm sorry."

"It's okay, Pekie. You don't have to face that creature again," Scout said, giving her shoulder a squeeze.

"I'll stay with you, Pekie," Amber said. "It might be too scary in there." She smothered her friend in a hug.

"Okay, then." Mildew and her volunteers headed inside. Captain Burroughs watched fascinated as she found the trigger and opened the door to the hidden passageway. She motioned for everyone to follow as she descended the stairs.

As if sensing their approach, the ghost let out a string of threats. The sound of items bouncing off walls caused even the bravest among them to shiver.

She poured a line of salt along the bottom of the doorway, then unlocked the door and pulled it open. An angry shimmer slammed into the invisible barrier the salt provided. The shimmer bounced back and a form appeared, waving its arms, flinging debris and dirt into the air. Then the ghost manifested into its most fierce strength and screamed *Let me out or I will—*.

"You will what?" Mildew asked in a loud voice. "The way I see it, you can't get out of this cramped little room."

You can't keep me here forever, George growled. He looked past her and zeroed in on Officer Elliott. *How's the shoulder?* he said, then laughed hideously.

"What the—" Officer Elliott started, but was too shocked to finish his thought.

"Shut up, ghost," Mildew yelled. She raised the bottle in her hand and let loose a spray of Holy Water. George seemed to diminish for a moment before raging back to growl in her face.

"I'm going to make you a one-time offer," Mildew said. "I want you to go into the light."

Like hell, George chuckled angrily. *I'm staying right here in my house.*

"It's not your house." Mildew put her hand in her pocket. "Perhaps you would be interested to know that we've located Miranda's remains. Also, as you may know, you left a little piece of yourself with her." She pulled the dirty root out of her pocket and held it up. "Your finger, I presume?"

He lunged toward her, but bounced off the salt barrier. *Give me that!*

"No, I have other plans for it," she said, slipping it back into her pocket.

She stared at him and he stared back, both waiting to see what would happen next, until George said, *What do you want?*

"You know what I want, and here's how I'm going to get it. I need an answer right now. I will summon the white light and you can go into it and experience whatever awaits you there, or I will take the piece of finger Miranda swallowed and I will burn it, and you will instantly wink out of existence. The choice is yours."

How do you know I will cease to exist?

"I don't, really, but are you willing to take the chance? What do you think has been holding you to this house all this time? That bitten off finger. I'll give you to three, George."

"One."

He growled and told her she would rot in hell.

"Two."

Nothing he did seemed to rattle the little round woman, who stood her ground fiercely.

"Thr—"

Wait! George bellowed. *What if I don't want to go?*

"I'm about to say 'three,' George. When I do, the door will close, and soon you will cease to exist. What's your answer?"

Okay. If I accept your offer, what will happen to me over there?

"I have no way of knowing that. Is it better to find out, or just no longer be? You decide."

Mildew turned as if to leave, and George yelled, *I accept. Just do it.*

Mildew closed her eyes and held out her hands, concentration wrinkling her forehead. She turned her palms up and warmth emanated from her hands. The ghost seemed to focus on a spot in front of him, snarled once, stepped forward, and then he was gone.

A collective sigh of relief was audible from everyone who had witnessed the unbelievable event. In silence, they turned to go up the stairs and found Pekin and Amber standing on the top steps.

"I couldn't not be there for the end," Pekin said simply.

Scout rushed up the stairs and pulled her into his arms. "I'm really proud of you, Pekie."

Suddenly, all was right in Pekin's world.

Chapter Forty-Two

N OT THAT SHE WOULD SOON FORGET what she'd experienced, but Pekin's relief that it was all over lifted her spirits.

Before the police left Elmwood, Officer Elliott pulled Pekin aside to apologize for his behavior and skepticism. He also took down the names and location of George Trent's other victims.

Miranda's ring had once again been left in the car. No one had wanted to take the chance that George could get to her in any way. Pekin retrieved the velvet pouch and brought it into the parlor where her friends had convened. With trepidation, she loosened the silken cords and dumped the amethyst ring in the palm of her hand.

"Would you be able to make that light thing again for Miranda?" she asked Mildew.

"Of course, dear. I'm happy to make sure she can go into the light when she's ready."

Taking a breath, Pekin slipped on the ring.

A shimmer formed in the doorway. Miranda materialized, taking in the room. *What's happened?* she asked. *It feels different.*

"It *is* different," Pekin said. "Oh, Miranda, we found your body. We'll make sure to have a proper burial for you as soon as the police say it's okay. I'll tell your...your...What *is* Elonia to Miranda?" Before anyone could answer, Pekin shrugged. "Whatever. Elonia is related to you, Miranda, and you probably have other relatives, too, who'll want to come to your funeral. And, by the way, Mildew banished George. He went into the light, which is more than he deserved."

Miranda clasped her hands, smiling a brilliant smile that lit up the room in spite of the fact that she was translucent. *So what happens now?*

"That would be up to you, dear," Mildew said. "You can cross over now, or you can wait until your funeral and leave after that."

Oh, Miranda said. *I don't know.*

"One more thing you might like, dear, is that you are no longer bound to either this house or the ring. You are actually free to go wherever you desire."

Miranda smiled and vanished, leaving surprised faces to wonder where she could have gone.

"You guys." Scout beckoned everyone to the window, pointing to a slightly vague young girl skipping along the sidewalk, spinning, her skirt swirling around her legs, eager to see everything that was so different a century after her death.

"I'm kinda troubled," Scout said to Mildew. "Why did George get to go into the light? It seems wrong that he gets to go to heaven, the same heaven as Miranda. Did you have to send him there?"

"Scout, I don't know what happens to the spirits who go into the light. It isn't necessarily a doorway to heaven. There could be judgment awaiting him, maybe an escort to take him to where he belongs. It's not for us to know. If he didn't go into the light, he would still be here on this plane, and possibly be able to continue his reign of terror."

"But what you said about burning his finger—"

"Might have worked. Or might not have worked. On TV shows like 'Supernatural,' burning the bones of evil entities banishes them to hell, but that solution may have bubbled up from someone's imagination. It wasn't worth the risk. Even if we could have had the finger returned to us, and, even if they agreed to return it, it would probably have been months, even years, before we had it back. Again, what if George managed to escape? His finger is no longer here, so he could have gone somewhere else to wreak havoc. I think this was the most appropriate outcome."

"Okay. I can live with that," he said.

"Let's go home," Pekin said. "It's been a long day." She ushered her friends out of Elmwood and locked the door behind them. "It will be a relief to give this key back to Elonia."

Chapter Forty-Three

"THE POLICE LOCATED those three missing girls," Mildew said. She had suggested a meeting with the Ghosties to talk about what they'd been through. "I talked to Captain Burroughs this morning. They're doing DNA testing on them, and on Miranda and George. They had to track down family members for all of them to see if they can get a familial DNA match."

"I'm glad," Pekin said. "No one should be lost forever. I'm hoping they can all find peace now."

"Except for George's family," Scout said. "Imagine finding out you have a serial killer for a relative. Even a long-dead one."

"So, I have some thoughts for you all," Mildew said. "Advice, actually. If you're going to try this again."

"I'm not sure," Pekin said. "Maybe I'm not cut out for this ghost stuff."

Scout put an arm around her shoulders. "I don't blame you, Pekie. You had it a lot worse than we did."

"Been there, done that, got the nightmares." She shivered.

"But look what we did," Amber said. "We solved four murders."

"You certainly did," Mildew said.

"So, what advice would you have for us?" Scout asked. "Just in case."

"First, I want to congratulate you all on what you accomplished. Not just anyone could have done it. The fact that you were able to connect with a spirit like that...It's very rare. I think with a little guidance you could be very talented."

"All of us?" Amber asked. "I mean, Pekin, of course. But what did we do...I mean, *I* do, that was so important?"

"You were open to the possibility, and you were welcoming. Not many ghosts allow themselves to be seen. Even you, Amber, can get good at this."

Amber beamed. "Thank you. I didn't think I was anything special."

"You're all special. You make a good team."

"We appreciate it," Scout said, "but tell us what you think we should know."

"Why could so many people see Miranda?" Pekin interrupted. "Usually, no one but me could see a ghost, but Miranda practically shook hands with everyone. It doesn't make sense."

"Hmm." Mildew bit her bottom lip. "I think it was Miranda's choice. Most ghosts don't want to be seen. Some of them like to be spooky and content themselves with rattling chains and slamming doors. Miranda, and George, had a hundred years to grow, to learn what they were capable of."

"But don't a lot of ghosts want to be seen by their loved ones when they pass away?"

"I believe they do, but they're too new to have developed any abilities. Most of them realize no one can see them, and they move on to the other side as they're supposed to."

"But Miranda—"

"It's only my opinion, of course. What I just said. I don't have all the answers. I'm sorry."

"It's okay," Pekin said. "I guess I'm just trying to understand."

"I don't think it's for us to know, my dear."

"Sorry for interrupting, you guys," Pekin said to Scout and Amber.

"No problem," Scout said. "So, what did you want to tell us?" he asked Mildew.

"There are just a few things," she responded. "First and most important, you should protect yourselves before you embark on a mission."

"How do we do that?" Pekin asked.

"Through prayer. You need to ask for a white light to surround you. It keeps spirits from attaching to you."

"You mean like what happened to Pekin with George?" Amber asked.

"No, that was a little different. It's so lesser entities can't harm you. I can show you how to protect yourselves. Second, and, Amber, don't take this personally but Holy Water is kind of a no-no. It makes ghosts mad."

"Oh, no. You mean everything that happened to Pekin was my fault?"

"Not precisely, but you said he got enraged after you sprayed him."

"I'm so sorry, Pekin. I didn't know." Amber suppressed a sob.

"It wasn't your fault," Pekin said soothingly. "None of us really knew what we were doing."

"But you used the Holy Water on George when we were in the storage room," Scout said.

"I did. I wanted to get a reaction from the ghost. To throw him off balance. But, in the future Amber doesn't need to steal any more of it."

"But I—"

"Everything happens for a reason," Mildew continued. "Because of George invading Pekin, four spirits will find peace now. Their families will finally have closure. Do you think there was any way, *any* way, the police would have solved those murders?"

"No, I don't suppose they would have. I'm glad *something* good came of it," Amber said.

"All in all," Mildew said, "your first case was a roaring success."

"And our college apps are going to be killer," Scout said. "Pardon the pun."

"There's something else we need to do before you tell your client the ghosts are gone," Mildew said. "We must cleanse the house."

"You mean dust and vacuum? Like that?" Pekin asked.

"No. Certain herbs and objects such as feathers contain strong healing, perhaps magical, properties. I use sage to remove any remaining negative energy. The house will be clean and ready for whatever the owner chooses to do with it."

Pekin looked pensive. "We should talk to Miranda," she said. "See if she wants to spend any time in Elmwood before you do the sage thing. She probably won't be able to enter it afterward."

"Yes, she might want to say goodbye to her home," Amber said. "It must be so weird for her to think about going to heaven."

"It's kinda weird for all of us," Scout said. "Pekie, can you get her to come talk to us?"

"I'll try, but now that she's free, who knows where she is. Let's see what happens." She put the amethyst ring on her finger and called to Miranda.

Miranda shimmered into their midst. She looked happy.

"Hi," Pekin said. "Are you okay? What have you been doing?"

I've been all over Springdale. I went to my old school, but it's not there any longer. Everything is so different. Your cars are so...modern. And the way people dress. Girls show so much of themselves. Tiny short pants, tops that cover so little. Nothing is as it was.

"Does that make you sad?" Amber asked.

A little, I think. It's so unlike what my life was.

"Ahem," Mildew said. "We need to talk to you about something, Miranda. Now that George has left the building, and you're free to go wherever you want, we will be cleansing Elmwood to purify the house, to bring good energy to it. I don't believe you will be able to enter the house after that point."

"We thought you might want to go through Elmwood and, I don't know, say goodbye or something," Amber said.

Yes. I would like to say goodbye. She looked sad.

"We're not kicking you out, Miranda," Pekin said. "But it's been long enough, hasn't it? Aren't you ready to see what's ahead for you? Be with your family?"

The ghost shrugged. She smoothed her hands over the skirt of her dress.

"Let's go to Elmwood and you can go through it one last time," Pekin said. "We can talk about what happens after that later. Deal?"

Yes. Deal.

"It's getting late, so let's plan to meet at Elmwood tomorrow," Mildew said. "Miranda, if you want, you could go early tomorrow and have time to yourself."

I'd like that, she said, her voice somber. Then she was gone.

MILDEW LEFT, WITH AMBER right behind her. Only Scout was left with Pekin. She was nervous and embarrassed, not sure what to say, until he scooted closer to her on the sofa and put an arm around her shoulders.

"Is this okay?" he asked, looking as nervous as Pekin felt.

She snuggled under his arm and glanced up at him. And blushed. "Yes."

They sat side by side quietly for a short while, feeling unsure about the new closeness between them.

Scout cleared his throat. "So, what do we do now?"

"Now?"

"Yeah. You and me. Do we, um, go on a date or something?"

"I'd like that."

"Great." He stood up. "I should go. So you can, you know… You're probably tired."

"Oh. I…yes."

Pekin stood and after an awkward moment hugged him. Her awkwardness lessened as he hugged her back, and didn't let go right away.

When he pulled away he said, "We should probably give Elonia her keys back."

"We should. I'll see if she wants to meet us at Elmwood after the cleansing tomorrow."

"Good idea." He turned to go, but hesitated and turned back. "Would you like to go out with me on Saturday? We could get something to eat and go to a movie?"

"Yes. Definitely." Pekin's smile lit up her whole face. "I'd love to."

Chapter Forty-Four

~~~~~~

P EKIN FOUND THE NEWSPAPER open on the kitchen table when she came down in the morning. The house was empty, and she was relieved not to have to talk to anyone.

SPRINGDALE POLICE, WITH ASSISTANCE FROM LOCAL TEENS, SOLVE CENTURY-OLD MURDERS. FOUR VICTIMS CAN FINALLY REST IN PEACE.

She sank into a chair and read the headline twice.

She texted Amber and Scout to check out the morning paper, including a snapshot of the front page, then poured a glass of orange juice and sat down at the table to read the article.

Of course, the police toned down the story. They indicated that evidence was found in an old house. They said the kids were doing some home renovations for the owner when they stumbled on a secret passageway and basement room. It said they contacted the police because they knew that a child had been kidnapped from the house decades ago and thought maybe the police might find some clues. No word on the ghost stuff, of course.

Chapter Forty-Five

WHEN AMBER AND SCOUT STOPPED to pick Pekin up, she noticed multiple copies of the newspaper on the back seat. Pekin pointed at the papers, a big smile on her face. "We're *famous*."

"Now can I tell Josh about everything?" Amber asked. "He's going to want details. All the ghosts are gone now, right?"

Pekin's brow scrunched up. "I don't know—"

"She's right, Pekie," Scout said. "Our friends will be asking questions. If we don't want to tell the truth, then we should get our stories straight about what we're going to tell people."

"And what if reporters want to talk to us? Or the morning shows. Or '20/20?'" Amber asked excitedly.

"I hadn't thought about that," Pekin said, tapping a finger on her chin.

"I really want to tell Josh," Amber said. "I haven't told him anything all this time. Besides, if we're advertising that we have a ghost business, it won't exactly be a secret."

"Can you at least ask him not to tell everyone?"

"I will. I promise."

Mildew's compact car pulled up to the curb and parked behind Scout. She clambered out carrying a shopping bag and joined the kids on the lawn in front of the house.

"Everyone ready?" she asked brightly.

"Come on," Pekin said as she unlocked the front door and pushed it open.

The moment they were inside, Amber asked, "Is it cold in here?"

"Are you here, Miranda?" Pekin called out. She was answered by a disembodied *Yes*, followed by a shimmer that evolved into the ghost of

Miranda standing with her back to the parlor windows, sunbeams and dancing dust motes visible through her transparent image.

"Did you say your goodbyes?" Mildew asked. "There's no rush if you need more time."

Miranda looked anxious, but said, *I don't need more time. There's really nothing left for me here.* She turned in a circle, a far off look on her face.

In the parlor, Mildew was preoccupied taking items out of her shopping bag, setting them gently on one of the sofa cushions.

What happens to me now? Miranda asked fearfully. *Do I just vanish on my own?*

"No, dear. I will make a light for you, a portal, and you can enter it. It will take you to the other side."

What will I do then?

"I believe your loved ones will be there to greet you. They'll know just what to do."

Oh.

"Wouldn't you love to see your parents again, dear?"

Yes. Of course. But what if they don't come for me?

"That would be very unusual. I'm sure they've all been waiting for you."

"Are you ready to cross over, Miranda?" Pekin asked gently.

Miranda looked torn, then sighed. *I missed so much of the life I should have had. I've been happy for the first time since meeting you all.* She paused and looked down. *What if...Could I stay?*

The question took everyone off guard. Finally, Pekin spoke.

"I don't know," she said. "Elonia Collins...she owns the house now...she probably will want to sell it. A new family will live here."

Maybe I could help with your cases. Maybe I could be a Ghostie like you.

"Um, I'm not sure." Pekin turned to Mildew. "What do you think?"

"Not everyone wants to go when they have the chance. She *has* missed a lot. Maybe if she hadn't been introduced to the modern world she would be eager to cross over to be with the loved ones she remembered. But now she may be curious." Looking a Miranda, she said, "Is that it, dear?"

Miranda looked down and shrugged, obviously embarrassed.

"Where would she go, since she probably can't stay at Elmwood?" Amber asked.

"She can think herself anywhere. Anywhere in the world. She doesn't have to *stay* anywhere."

Miranda looked up. *Really?* she asked hopefully.

"Yes, I believe so," Mildew replied. "You're not bound by the laws of the physical world."

"We haven't really discussed whether *we* still want to be Ghosties," Pekin said.

Scout and Amber looked at her. "We don't?" Amber asked.

"Would we want to go through something like that again?" Pekin asked softly.

Scout squeezed her hand. "Only you can answer that question, Pekie. You bore the brunt of what happened at Elmwood. If you're too freaked out—"

"I don't know that I'm freaked out. I don't know what I am."

Is it my fault? Miranda asked, concern on her face.

"No, no. You weren't the evil one, Miranda. You were a victim. You're blameless. What happened to me...if I'm being honest, I brought it on myself. I had to twist some arms to get Scout and Amber on board. I *really* twisted those arms."

"We can talk about it later," Scout said. "I admit, though, it was an eye-opening experience for me. I'd be willing to give it another go if anyone else wants to."

"Me, too," Amber said. "Can you believe I just said that?"

"I almost feel like laughing," Pekin admitted. "Let's think about it overnight and we can get together in the morning and decide what we want to do."

"Sounds good," Amber said.

"If you would like any input from me," Mildew said. "I'd be happy to help. This life isn't for everyone, you know." She rubbed her hands together. "Now, should we get started?"

Pekin noticed Miranda watching in fascination, and smiled at the ghost. "I wanted to tell you, Miranda, I'm going to have your ring buried with you. I know you loved it. Now that you aren't bound to the ring, I think it should be with your remains."

Thank you, the ghost replied.

"Do you want your doll buried with you, too? The one in the closet upstairs?

Her name is Arabella. Yes, please. Can she be with me, too? Thank you again.

"Of course we'll bury Arabella with you. We'll make sure she's all cleaned up and as pretty as she ever was. If you're ready, we're going to cleanse the house now. You should probably wait outside."

Miranda nodded and vanished.

Mildew gathered the three teens and, bowing her head, said a prayer asking for protection and help in clearing any remaining spirits from Elmwood, then waved her sage bundle away from her body, sending the aromatic smoke floating into each corner and up to the ceiling. After watching Mildew in action, Pekin, Amber and Scout each selected a room of their own to cleanse. After half an hour, the job was complete.

"Hellooo," called a voice from the foyer. A brightly colored Elonia Collins put a hand on the banister and called, "Yoo hoo. Anyone here?"

"We're upstairs," Pekin called. "Be right down."

Elonia handed Pekin a check when everyone was in the parlor and introductions had been made. She glanced around the room and sniffed. No one mentioned the sage.

"I suppose you've seen the news articles," Pekin said with pride. "We found Miranda's remains, and she no longer haunts your house. It should be good for whatever you intend to do with it."

"I read them with interest. Did you actually see Miranda's ghost?" Elonia's eyes were big.

"Yes. It was through clues she gave us that we were able to tell the police where they could find her body."

"What was it like, seeing a ghost? I wish I'd seen it. Were you afraid?"

"Maybe a little scared at first, but Miranda didn't want to hurt anyone. It was an interesting experience and everything worked out for the best." Pekin gave Elonia a short rundown of the events leading up to the discovery of Miranda's remains, leaving out any mention of her own experience with George Trent. Before Elonia could gush any further or ply them with questions, Pekin said, "Thank you for the check. It's been a pleasure doing business with you."

She handed Elonia the old key and Pekin, Scout, Amber, and Mildew all escaped out the front door, very happy to leave Elmwood behind.

"Would you want to meet with us tomorrow?" Pekin asked Mildew. "We probably have a ton of questions. Maybe that would help us decide what we want to do."

Could I come, too? Miranda suddenly appeared in their midst.

"You really don't want to go?" Scout asked her.

I want to hear the rest of Harry Potter, she said.

"That could take a long time," Pekin said with a laugh. "There are seven books."

"Or," Scout offered, "we could watch the DVDs."

EPILOGUE

~~~~~~

S OMBER EXCITEMENT WAS IN THE AIR the day of Miranda's funeral. It felt like an end. Which it was, in a way.

The small pink coffin sat on a platform at the front of the church, a refreshed and clean Arabella and an amethyst ring tucked in beside the remains.

The pastor had been informed that Pekin wanted to say a few words on behalf of Miranda, so at his invitation she made her way to the podium, with a smile and a wink for Miranda.

"We're here today to lay to rest a young girl whose life was tragically taken far too soon. She was missed by her loved ones. I'd like to read a letter from her mother that conveys their pain and loss. Miranda wasn't the only victim of the vicious George Trent. But I don't speak today of the three other girls that George Trent took away, because this day is about Miranda. The other victim I refer to is her family, who were devastated as well, and never recovered from the grief that must have haunted them the remainder of their lives."

She unfolded a copy of the letter Elizabeth Talbert had written to her daughter Miranda almost a century ago. As she read, sniffles could be heard from the assembled mourners.

Pekin cleared her throat and continued with her eulogy. "Miranda, you'll never be forgotten. Even though I never met you in person, I feel like I know you. I was lucky enough to be part of the team that discovered where your body was hidden all these years. God bless you, dear girl. You'll be part of our lives forever."

She glanced at Miranda as she took her seat. There were ghost tears streaking Miranda's cheeks, and her chin trembled. *Thank you*, she said. *For saving me.*

Pekin nodded. "It was my pleasure."

Pekin's phone vibrated in her pocket. She chanced a quick glance at it, but didn't recognize the number, so she hit the "Ignore" button and slipped it back into her pocket.

It was only later, at home, that she noticed the voicemail.

"Ms. Dewlap. I wondered if you're taking new clients."